COAST TO COAST

Arizona Raptors, book 1

_____

RJ SCOTT
VL LOCEY

Love Lane Books

Copyright

Dedication

To my family who accepts me and all my foibles and quirks. Even the plastic banana in my holster.
VL Locey

Always for my family,
RJ Scott

COAST to COAST

RJ SCOTT &
V.L. LOCEY

ONE

Mark

MY BROTHERS ARE both older than me, and loving the two of them is impossible at the best of times. Ten years ago they turned their backs on me, and I want to forgive them, but I can't.

Jason was the eldest son, hair as curly and dark as mine, his eyes that same deep Westman-Reid brown he and I had inherited from my asshole of a dad. Big brother one was currently sitting in the chair behind Dad's old desk, looking as if someone had pissed in his Wheaties, and tapping a pen rhythmically on the leather blotter. I didn't think he was that happy, but then, he'd been the one closest to Dad, the golden boy, so I guessed Dad dying was a big downer in his charmed life.

Cameron was the middle son, and I know the books said that the middle children are supposed to be the negotiators, the ones to placate their siblings with kind words. Only Cam was not doing that right now. He was pacing, throwing things, and I imagined his personal grief was manifesting itself in the glorious temper that also came from my dad. He looked more like Mom, blond, blue eyes, kind of pretty, but not quirky or fey enough for my modeling agency to book him.

"You want what? You're both mad. Over my dead fucking body will I stay here and work with you. No." I was horrified. I didn't drop the F-bomb much in general, but what they'd just said was enough to have me using fuck as punctuation.

"Say that again!" Cameron snapped, right in my face. "I dare you."

Never let it be said that I am the kind of man who backs down on a dare. Last time someone had dared me to do something, I'd ended up getting arrested, and pictures of my naked butt appeared all over social media.

"No," I repeated. That wasn't a no about the dare; that was a nod to the proposal that I work with my brothers for a year on their failing hockey team.

"No! The fucker said no." Cam was apoplectic and began pacing the office again, going from one end where Dad had kept his vinyl record collection, and finishing at the other where the family portrait hung, before repeating this all over again. Of course, that meant I looked at the painting—Mom sporting the Westman-Reid diamonds, elegant in a sapphire ball gown that matched her eyes, and Dad in a morning suit. To the left was Jason appearing to be around twenty or so, looking like the prep school Ivy League asshole he'd always been. To the right Cam, cute even then, and with not one hint of temper in his expression. Then there was me, sitting on the arm of a chair, aged twelve and fully aware then that I didn't belong in the painting. Leigh wasn't in the picture, typical hypocritical Westman-Reid shit. Clearly having the child in the wheelchair in the painting would've detracted from my dad's sheer awesomeness or some such shit. Funny how I'd never noticed she wasn't in the picture.

Four years after this painting, I was told to leave the mansion. I guessed I was lucky that Dad hadn't cut me out of the painting as brutally as he had cut me out of his life.

"You realize so much will be lost if you don't agree," Jason was calm as if talking to me sensibly might get me to change my mind.

I crossed one leg over the other, pulling at my pants until the crease fell just so. I took pride in my clothes, but the move was more of a delaying tactic than sustaining my tailored elegance.

"That's not my problem," I said.

The chair I sat on rocked violently as Cam smacked the back of it. "Not your problem? Do you know how much the team would lose?"

I guessed the question was rhetorical, but I couldn't stay quiet. "So your kids have to have loans for college, and you don't get to vacation on an island in the Bahamas. Sucks to be you."

"Jesus Christ, you're a fucking asshole," Cam exploded, and placing a hand on either side of the arms of my chair, he then leaned right into my face—so close I could see the darker blue in his eyes and imagined the scarlet lightning of temper exploding from them at any minute. "Do you have any idea of what you're talking about?"

I peered around him in my most deliberate fashion and stared at Jason. "Are you going to get him out of my face, or do I need to call 911?"

"Cam, back down," Jason ordered, and finally after a staring match that seemed to last hours, Cam threw his hands in the air and resumed pacing.

"Many people depend on the Raptors to be able to support their families," Jason explained in his level-headed way.

"You can't guilt me into this, Jason. Dad threw me out

at sixteen, with no money, no idea of what to do, and I hitchhiked my way to New York. I worked my butt off to make something of myself there, and Gilded Treasures is more than enough to support over three hundred staff and models. I made something of myself despite dear old Dad, and I owe this family nothing."

"What about Mom?" Cam snapped.

"The same woman who stood next to Dad and watched him kick me out, then ignored my calls and cut me out of her life as efficiently as if she'd used a blade?"

"She's not well," Jason said, tiredly.

A small prick of concern pierced the act I had going on, but I wasn't going to let it sway me. She had washed her hands of me a long time ago, and she meant nothing to me now. I pushed aside that traitorous sympathy and focused back on Cam and Jason. "Maybe she should stop drinking," I said.

That was clearly the wrong thing to say. Cam dragged me out of the chair and walked me backward until I hit a wall. He lifted me onto my toes, easy when he was built like a linebacker with all the physical qualities of the Incredible Hulk.

"Mom has cancer," he said, and that poke of concern became slightly bigger.

"Cameron, stop," Jason ordered and pushed his way between us. I'm not sure why he was stopping Cam from beating me up. He'd never done it when we were kids, so why now? "She didn't want him to know," he said as he shoved Cam backward.

Yep, and there it is, the cherry on the icing of the proverbial shit cake. I brushed myself down.

"Of course, she doesn't want me to know. She probably assumed I don't care, and she was right." I feigned a complete lack of concern, but even after all these years, it was her betrayal that hurt the most.

Cam moved in front of me, although he kept his distance.

"She didn't want her illness to sway you one way or another with what Dad put in motion."

I looked at my nails and huffed. "And that's the story she's sticking to, right?"

Cam slammed a hand into the wall next to my head. He was taller and bigger than me, just like Jason, and if the two of them decided to take it upon themselves to kill me, they could. At five ten, I was completely vulnerable.

I wasn't the same stupid kid who'd left the house at sixteen. Not the one who'd adored Cameron and admired him as if he was a shiny, heroic genius. Or who'd been the only one to stop Jason from losing his cool all the time.

I was Mark Westman-Reid, twenty-six, owner of a thriving modeling agency, an apartment, with a scarlet Lamborghini parked outside the mansion to prove it. Not to mention owning a loft looking out over Central Park or having a Porsche that sat in the garage as a spare.

That Mark was a very different person, and my brothers needed to know that.

"One year," Cameron said and closed his eyes briefly.

"What about Leigh? What is our sister's role in this?"

Jason and Cam exchanged looks, and I'd have even gone as far as to say they both appeared regretful.

"You know Dad just wanted to look after her," Cam said finally. Then he changed the subject. "One year as part owner of the Raptors is all the will states. The three of us can fulfill the conditions of Dad's will, and we'll buy you out."

"Buy me out? Huh. What with?"

The family had invested in the Arizona team before I'd

left home, and even though I wasn't a hockey fan, I was a businessman, with advisors and investors, and my own goddamn corner office. I knew business, and I didn't have to be a fan of hockey in general or the Raptors themselves to see that the team was failing.

Their eighteen-thousand seating capacity Santa Catalina Arena was barely forty percent full on good nights, and the players were in and out of trouble about as often as Cam had been as a kid. They were close to the bottom of the league, and their reputation was shit among the other teams. There was violence, a couple of DUIs, rumors of steroid abuse, and worst of all, no franchise wanted to set up stalls in the place for game nights. All of that I'd read in one article on the NHL website.

They'd had some good picks for the last draft, and clicking on both those links had given me a good understanding of what that meant. The team had picked up a couple of good rookies. Other than that, they'd made no changes to the players.

Worst of all, it seemed the team had one player who was a mean son of a bitch who'd gone out of his way to hurt the league's darling, Tennant Rowe, which meant that now the Arizona Raptors were the bad guys.

They were fucked six ways to Sunday. The latest article on the Raptors' website talked about a last-minute coach hired from an east-coast college with no NHL-level experience at all. Dad had to have been desperately scraping the bottom of the barrel for that. Money breeds money, and Rowen something or other wasn't going to save a team hell-bent on self-destruction.

And Dad had wanted his three sons to work together for a year? Why? What the hell reason could he have for making us do this? If we didn't, then the last of Dad's money was going to charity, and the team would be wound up. Finished. And it was doubtful that it could be sold on to any other unsuspecting schmuck.

"We have financing in place if we need it," Jason defended, but I'd forgotten what I even asked. I was done here, and for my own sanity, I needed to leave.

"No," I repeated and slipped out of the room. They didn't follow me, but I could hear the rumble of voices behind the door.

"What did you say?"

I turned to face Leigh with a smile and leaned down to give her a hug. Leigh was the only true innocent in all of this, and I wished I could say that I'd kept in touch with her, but I'd have been lying. The oldest of all four of us, she'd been a passenger in a car accident aged five and was confined to a wheelchair. I don't remember much about her growing up. She'd been this ghost who'd passed through my life on her way to rehabs or for operations. At least she hadn't been next to Dad when he'd thrown me out, though, and I had affection for her, just not the kind that was enough for me defy my father and keep in touch.

Not even as a grown-ass man had I reached out. That was on me. Maybe now he was gone, I could think about visiting her. On days when my asshole brothers weren't there, of course. Or Mom. God forbid I bump into my mom.

"I said no," I was honest and to the point.

She half smiled, then wheeled herself down the hall to the front door, and I followed. "I thought you would. You don't owe us anything."

"I don't feel a part of this family," I murmured. "You get that, right?"

"Likewise," she said and smiled again. She was another blonde, like Mom and Cam, and was so pretty. *I wonder how she's doing?* Had she ended up at college? What was her role in the family, apart from the one everyone looked after? And why did I feel as if I was abandoning her. "Did they tell you about Mom?"

I nodded. The part of my brain processing the news was mostly taken up by the fact that I'd decided my position on the Raptors situation, and I was sticking to it.

"Not that it matters," she added.

"Huh?"

"Part of her died with Daddy." She held out a hand, and I took it without hesitation. "You know, the part where she couldn't make her own choices, the part that Dad made her lock down, her life, her joy, her painting. It's crappy timing that the moment he dies and sets her free is the same time she gets cancer. Life sucks, you know."

I crouched down next to her and looked up. "Mom didn't care about me. Our brothers stood by and let Dad cut me out of this family. I've lost that spark of love for the way they represent family. Do you understand?"

"I'm in a wheelchair. I'm not stupid," she said wryly.

I felt embarrassed at the way I'd worded my question. "Sorry, I didn't mean…"

"I'm teasing you. Did you know you have three nieces and two nephews?"

"You send me the family newsletter every year, sis."

"Emma, Lucy, Ewan, Michael, and Gemma," she counted them off on her fingers. "I bet they'd love to meet their uncle Mark."

"The roaming gay uncle who made a living stripping his clothes off for money?"

She shook her head. "No. The successful businessman who started as a model, who made curly hair famous, and now runs his own modeling agency, owns an apartment overlooking Central Park, and drives a Lamborghini." She waved at the shiny red car, and I sat next to her on the short wall of the porch, feeling as if this conversation had a purpose. "You have a business manager, right?"

"Lucas."

"Let him run your company. He could cover you being on the west coast. You know the will only stipulates two hundred working days spread over the year. You could be more to your nieces and nephews. You could take me out for dinner. We could talk about our past, maybe look forward to our future. You never know, you might one day forgive Mom and Jason, and maybe there will be a miracle, and you could even be friends with Cam. But you won't know that unless you give us all a chance."

"I don't know anything about hockey."

"I don't imagine that getting kicked out of your home and onto the streets with no money meant you knew a damn thing about modeling either, but look at you now."

"I don't like the cold."

"We live in Arizona."

"Ice is cold."

"I'll lend you a jersey."

The banter was a hundred kinds of cute, and an overwhelming rush of self-pity stole my breath. She must have seen it in my face, and she patted my head.

"Come on, Mark, give this family issue a week. Take it a day at a time. We can go out for a beer. We can watch hockey together. I'd like to get to know my little brother again."

"What about Mom?"

"She's away right now, at an all-inclusive spa in Sedona. She went there with a trunk of books, three cases of wine, and it's closer to the clinic she's attending. She's grieving over losing Dad at her own pace."

"What kind of cancer does she have?"

"Breast cancer."

"Did she know about this insane clause in Dad's will?"

Leigh shrugged. "I wouldn't be surprised if she encouraged him to put it in there."

"What do you mean?"

"Now's not the time to talk about all that, Mark. Now is the time to go back into the office, calm Cam down, and talk to Jason rationally. See if there's something you can get started. Do it for the family that fucked you over, show them you're the bigger man, come home for a while and be Uncle Mark."

She held out a hand, and I gripped it, pressing a kiss to her knuckles.

"I wish you'd been home more when…"

"Yeah." She shook her head sadly. "Me too."

I WALKED BACK into the office without knocking and took a mental picture of what I was looking at. Cam at the window, arms crossed over his chest, staring out at the manicured lawns of the Westman-Reid estate. Jason slumped in the chair I'd been sitting in, pale and almost appearing as if he was going to cry.

"One week," I announced, and both men were startled out of wherever their thoughts had taken them. "I'm giving this one week, but I have conditions." I sat on the edge of Dad's desk and glanced between my brothers, both of whom wore mirrored looks of bewilderment.

"What conditions?" Cam asked and uncrossed his arms.

"My own office, access to every scrap of financial data for the past ten years, personal meetings with every single player, links to game film, someone to explain the rules of the game, and a place for Leigh to work with us if she wants to. That's nonnegotiable. If we want to turn this team around, then as part of this management team of three, we cut out all the deadwood: the skaters who don't give a shit, the managers getting fat skimming from the meager income we make. And most of all, we negotiate with this new coach, whatever his name is—"

"Rowen Carmichael."

"Him. We tell him to get the hell out and find a team at his level."

"He's already in place at the arena, and Dad gave him a loophole-free contract," Cam warned.

I fronted both of them. "I don't give a shit about a loophole-free contract."

"Mark—"

I held up a hand. "No negotiation on any of this. I want a real coach, not some half-assed college wannabe. I want Rowen Carmichael gone."

TWO

Rowen

WAKING up in a new bed with the sun shining in my face could've been poetic. Maybe. If the mattress wasn't too soft. I rolled to my side to get the desert sun out of my eyes, and my spine snapped with short, loud cracks as if someone had just fired up a popcorn popper.

"Ouch, fuck," I groaned. First thing on the agenda after a run was finding a new mattress. Yes, I was being ungrateful. Sue me. The team had provided a rather nice apartment with a cactus right outside on my patio and all the furnishings, and one perk that I'd requested—a big-screen TV. That was all I cared about for my downtime—a widescreen for viewing Aragorn and Bilbo, Luke and Leia, Aslan and Jadis, Jon and Tyrion. Obviously, I'd overlooked the need for an extra-firm mattress. I'd fix that today after morning skate.

The alarm on my phone went off. I sat up, slid from under the covers, then padded to the window and let the sun warm my face. The buzzing of my phone died down. Eyes closed, I basked, my lips parted, and my throat exposed. Sure, the sun might cause a few more wrinkles.

So what? I was over forty now and not looking to impress anyone. Although it *would've* been nice to have someone to share the rush of this monumental moment in my career with. Someone who didn't think I was making the single worst decision ever. Even worse than my decision to date Carl back in college, according to my sister.

God, Carl had been a simpleton. Spoiled, rich, hung up on the aesthetic of everything, vapid, and lost in the beauty of his own face and the faces of others. Aspiring model. Incredibly beautiful but lacking any redeemable value at all. I'd learned quickly that wealthy pretty boys were not my thing unless it was a quick hookup. Otherwise, I kept a wide berth from men who placed the value of beauty over the more important attributes such as loyalty, patience, humor, and a solid work ethic.

My phone sounded again, ruining my morning moment in the sun. Smiling at the big green cactus with its arms raised skyward, I jogged over to where I'd left it, saw the incoming call, and rolled my eyes to the ceiling. One of the heirs. The eldest maybe? There was a slew of Westman-Reid children, at least four, which is a slew in my book. Anything over two is just showing off.

"Morning," I said into the phone as I rummaged around in my carry-on for a pair of shorts. My running shoes were in a box… somewhere in this new place of mine.

"Coach Carmichael, I'm happy to finally catch up with you. Seems you made quite a splash when you arrived yesterday."

I dug down deep into my bag and snagged my running shorts. "Just letting the players know where I stand." Now, where were my shoes? I turned in circles several times, looking at the boxes and bags piled up in the corners of my bedroom. I tucked the phone between my head and my shoulder and stepped into my shorts, tugging them up over a pair of black briefs.

"It sent a message. Listen, could we have a morning meeting at my parents' house, say nine or so?"

"Which kid is this again?"

"Jason. The eldest son."

"Ah." He sounded as if he were proud to be the oldest, like he'd done something special to earn his birth order. Rich boys. Such jerks. "Well, Jason, I can't do a meeting at nine. I'll be at the barn by eight." If I could find my fucking running shoes that was…

"Oh, I'm sorry, but I… the barn?"

"Yeah, the barn. The rink. The big oval place where they make ice and men with sticks skate on it in pursuit of a puck." A long silence followed my explanation. Aha! A box marked shoes! I hurried over to it and tugged the flaps open. There lay my Nikes. "I can see you around two in the afternoon. I have some things to discuss with you about player and coaching staff changes that need to be made."

"I, uhm, well, isn't it usually the owners and the general manager who—?"

"My input is guaranteed in the contract I signed with your father. If you want to turn this sideshow you call a team around, then you need to listen to me. I know this game, and I know what it takes to win," I said as I bounced around on one foot while pulling on a gray sneaker. "I'll see you at two. Send me directions."

I hung up, found my earbuds, pulled up the Eagles' *The Long One* album on my music app, used my nose spray, slid my left shoe on, and set off for a cool five-mile run to purge the whiny voice of Westman-Reid the Eldest Son out of my brain.

I WAS WAITING for the players when they arrived. Most gave me a meek smile as they entered the Raptors' dressing room; some seemed wary, others cocky as if they were unimpressed with me and my stupid blue broom. They'd all be feeling the bristles of the clean sweeping that was about to commence. Each man got a small jerk of my head to indicate they were to stand along the far wall, the one with "Play Hard, Play with Passion, Play to Win" running along near the ceiling. Pretty words. Shame the team had no clue how to put any of that into practical application. All this team knew was strife and chaos. I could feel the discord in the locker room.

When everyone had lined up, I stepped forward, wearing my new Raptors jacket and my shiny whistle dangling around my neck.

"Morning, gentlemen, today is the first day of Raptors training camp. Today is also the first day of your time under me." I walked back and forth in front of my men, thin tablet in hand, making eye contact with every player I passed. I could learn a lot from looking into a man's eyes. "I'll be running you all through conditioning sprints today, so I hope you all ate your Wheaties."

They all grumbled, which was nothing out of the ordinary. All the players hated the assessment drills. Speed sprints were killer; I knew that. I'd skated them fifteen years in a row during my time with Montreal. Such was life for a hockey player.

"Before we hit the ice, I'd like all the rookies to step forward," I said, then stood at the end of the row of beefy men. Five players broke from the ranks. Five fresh-faced young lads with the glow of youth on their smooth cheeks. They all seemed edgy as if they thought I might flog them or something. "You five will join me for dinner tonight. I'll buy a new grill, since grilling is the only cooking I can do well. I'll text you the place and time." There were nervous titters from the five rookies. The vets were trying to figure out what I was all about. They'd find out given time.

"Okay, hit the gym, then be on the ice at nine sharp." I glanced at the big round clock over the door. The one with the fierce-looking hawk clutching a hockey stick in its talons. "And a heads-up, I loathe people being late. Being late is a sign of disrespect, and I will not be disrespected. Anyone showing up late once will find their ass taking part in a bag skate. If you show up late twice in one season, your ass will sit out a game. If you show up late three times, your ass will be sent down to the minors."

Eyes flared as wide as dinner plates, rookies and vets alike. No one said a word, though they all stared and bobbed their heads. I left them there against the wall and went off in search of my new office. It was a bleak little space by the therapy room, but it had been freshly painted, which was nice. A soft tan color with a red stripe that ran around the middle of the room. I'd brought a small box of personal items in today, and so after sending out a personal message to my fellow coaches, I began placing things around on the desk or on top of a bookshelf in the corner.

On the top of the small bookshelf, I put a picture of Anatoly Tarasov, a famous Russian bench boss with a finesse-over-force style. I arranged the image so that it faced the desk and I could see the quote attributed to him written over it when seated:

SPEED OF HAND, *speed of foot, speed of mind.*
Train for each of these, but never forget, the most important is speed of mind.

. . .

This was my coaching motto. Hockey was no longer a game of gorillas on skates itching for a fight. The game had evolved. Coaching had evolved with it. Some teams, it seemed, were still back in the early seventies—this one being a prime example. It was up to me and the people I had under me to drag the Raptors into this new era of speed of hand, foot, and mind. A sharp rap on the door jarred me from hockey philosophy. I called them in. Four men entered. I shook hands with them all, getting their names and positions. Video coach was Todd Walsh, defensive coach Craig Millerson, goalie coach Art Schaffer, and associate coach Pete Dunne.

"Thanks for coming. This won't take long." I rested my ass on the edge of my ugly metal desk, folded my arms over my spiffy new jacket, and stared directly at Pete Dunne. "Your services to this team are no longer required," I told Pete.

He stared openly at me for several long minutes. The other men looked up and down, side to side, any which way they could not to make eye contact with me.

"I have a contract," Pete coughed out.

"Which you will be released from." Pete gasped like a goldfish out of its bowl. "This team is changing direction. Your coaching technique does not jibe with our modern philosophy of five-man team systems, individual player skill, puck possession, and speed of mind. You've become mired in the old ways and allowed this creeping sickness that is team disharmony and low standards to flourish. So, as they say on *Drag Race*, sashay away."

"I have a contract!" He blustered and bellowed all the way home or more than likely to the general manager, who would call the owners. Which was fine. I'd tell the Gucci Boys the same thing I'd just told Pete. The other coaches waited with bated breath. "You're all safe. I've read over your résumés and have seen the effort you've been making. The old coach was a dinosaur. We're a bit more advanced."

"So, we're mammoths?" Todd, my defensive coach, tossed out, which broke the tension nicely. "My wife would agree. You should hear her bitching about the hair on my back."

We all had a nice chuckle over Todd's hairy back. I was thankful for the levity Todd had brought into the room. I tended to be kind of dry, according to several past lovers and my family. Also, direct, although why being direct was a bad thing, I didn't know. I thought being forthright was something rather admirable.

"Let's go run the players through their paces, shall we?" I motioned at the door Pete had left open. They all nodded, relief clear in their expressions.

I led them to the ice and then worked my new team into sweaty, gasping blobs on wobbly skates. The rookies were whipped, the veterans half-dead, but I now had a pretty good idea of who had spent the summer training and who had spent it loafing. Tomorrow, I'd start setting up preliminary lines and begin easing this team of bullies and cheap-shot kings into the Rowen Carmichael way of playing hockey.

After the players limped off the ice, I spent a good hour in my office, setting up my computer and touching base with the nearest Mattress Maven store in downtown Tucson. They assured me my new bed would arrive in an hour, so I went home to wait for the delivery. After it was in place and the old, soft, shitty thing hauled away, I put clean sheets on my new mattress, patted it, and grinned when it never moved. Like petting a hardwood floor. Perfect.

My fridge was barren, so I made a mental note to stop and shop on the way back from the Westman-Reid estate.

I'd need enough food and drink for hungry men. Lots of Dr Pepper—my favorite drink—and steaks, potatoes, and stuff for a big tossed salad. Maybe some bread and other staples as well. I prattled off a shopping list into my phone, then called for another ride. I'd also need a car. Something sporty maybe, since I wouldn't need to worry about crippling snow or ice storms. I could own a car without studded tires or chains or four-wheel drive. How exciting.

The driver, José, was a personable enough fellow, skinny with a soft Mexican accent, who whistled long and low when we were granted permission to enter the Westman-Reid grounds. Huge gates opened slowly, and José and I both gaped at the mansion rolling into view.

"Sweet Virgin Mary," José whispered.

"You can say that again," I replied, handing him his fare and a nice tip. He steered the Toyota carefully around a white Mercedes, a black BMW, a red Lamborghini, and a soft blue Porsche.

"Ostentatious much?" I asked all the cars parked in front of the sprawling manse. It was like walking into the set of *Dallas* or *Dynasty*. "Unreal," I mumbled, then went to knock on the ornate front door. It was pulled open by an older man in a dark suit. Obviously a butler, who bowed politely and fawned properly as he led me up a sweeping grand staircase to "the master's office" where I was left to dawdle in the hall like a waif.

I tugged my suit jacket down, removed the tie I'd put on, pulled my jeans up, and walked into the office without knocking. Three men and a lovely young woman in a wheelchair all gasped when I threw the door open and strolled in.

Two of the males were ordinary looking enough, dressed well of course, but lacking in any real appeal. The third one, seated in a wingback with one leg crossed over the other, was striking. And I mean the kind of striking that made a man pause just to admire him as one would a painting in the Louvre. He had deep brown eyes framed with thick dark lashes, a beautiful head of dark curls, and lips that were ripe and plump. His scruff was artfully done and his clothing top of the line but not screaming about how much it cost. A delicate gold watch on his slim wrist was the only accessory I noted. He was stunning. Pity he was one of the owner's whelps.

"Coach Carmichael, you're early," the big man behind the even bigger desk said as he rose to his feet. "Please come in and sit down. Can we ring the staff to bring you anything?"

"I'm fine," I replied, shaking the cool hand, then releasing it.

"Very well. Let's get to know each other. This is my brother Cameron, my sister Leigh, and my brother Mark." I nodded at them all, then sat in a fat leather chair about ten feet from Mark Westman-Reid. I could smell his cologne. It was heady and spicy with a hint of musk and floral. Nice. "We've been trying to keep up with you. You've created quite a stir since you arrived in Tucson."

Jason chuckled the way powerful men do when they think they're being funny. I arched an eyebrow. The titters died off.

"Did you seriously fire Pete Dunne without even consulting us?" Mark went straight for the jugular. "You can't—"

"Mark—" Jason interrupted him.

"—he can't do that kind of shit," Mark finished. He stood and moved toward me, looming over me, and I copied immediately. If there was a showdown, then I wanted to face it head on.

"I can. And I did. The man was a boil on the backside of professional hockey."

Leigh giggled, then quickly covered it with a tiny hand. Mark, he of the kissable lips, stared at me as if starfish were dancing on my head.

"You don't have the right to hire and fire at will." He was angry, "who do you think you are? You're the last person my dad should have hired."

Jason, Leigh, and Cameron sat quietly on the sidelines, so I guessed it was Mark who was leading this show.

"Please carry on." I wanted to hear all about why I wasn't suitable for the job I'd been hired for.

"You coached at a college."

Ah. So we were going straight *there*.

I held up a hand. "Irrespective of whether or not I should have been hired, my contract with your father has a proviso that gives me the right to hire and fire who I wish with regard to those serving under me." I let that sink in. "Please feel free to read over my contract and understand that I am here to stay."

"We will of course," Jason hurried to say after Mark began chewing his own tongue off in frustration. "But perhaps if you'd give us a heads-up with regards to your plans, we'd be able to—"

"Fine, I plan on flying out to Seattle at the end of the week to speak with the person I want to hire as my assistant coach."

All four Westman-Reid children sat in stunned silence. Had I said a bad word? I was an old hockey player; perhaps a stray F-bomb had fallen out of my mouth. Jason blinked as if he had sand in his eyes. Cameron's mouth fell open. Leigh sat primly in her wheelchair, bright eyes steady on me, and Mark with the huge brown eyes was so furious he couldn't seem to find the words.

"Did I stutter?" I asked when the silence dragged on.

"No, no, of course not, we just weren't…"

"No way are you going to Seattle to hire anyone," Mark snarled, his pretty eyes sparking with heat and passion. It was a look that did wonderful things for his already handsome features. Cameron and Jason began throwing words at Mark. Mark flung words back at his brothers. I rolled my eyes for Ms. Leigh, and she smiled sweetly at me.

"When you've finished, *boys*, I suggest you check my contract…" I remained as genial as I could manage. The Westman-Reids were no better than squabbling kids.

"I'm going with you," Mark said and crossed his arms over his chest, as if he'd won the entire argument.

I could've put my foot down. I could've told him to get the fuck out of my plans, but something in his eyes dared me to say no, and I never backed down from a dare.

"No skin off my nose," I said nonchalantly.

He loved that and pulled himself tall. "And I will approve any and all contracts offered."

"No."

"You have no say in this—"

"Now listen here, boy—"

"I'm not a boy!" Mark growled. No, he wasn't. I had to agree with that. Now that he was on his feet, it was clear he was all man. Lean yes, but nearly as tall as me. He lacked my bulk, but he wasn't scrawny or twinky.

"Sorry." He sniffed at my apology. "You're free to come along, but your input won't mean shit to me unless you know hockey. Do you?"

Mark's righteous indignation fled. "I know enough."

"Uh-huh. I'll be hiring who I deem to be a good fit for me and the vision of the team I'm building." I held out my arm, flicked my sleeve out of the way, and read my watch.

"Now, if you'll excuse me, I have to go buy groceries. I'm having the rookies over for dinner tonight."

I bowed to Ms. Leigh and walked out of the master's office, smiling to myself as the voices of the three Westman-Reid male heirs exploded into a heated discussion behind me.

THREE

Mark

I LAID out the screen prints I'd taken and pointed at them dramatically. Jason and Leigh immediately began to read what I'd found. Cameron paced because his temper was too high to do anything else but walk his path around the office.

Then I brooded. *Asshole coach called me a boy.*

When you're as old as him, anyone under thirty is a boy, but with only fifteen years between us, he could fuck right off with his insulting labels.

Even when we'd gone head to head, he hadn't been what I'd expected at all. He cut an intimidating figure, and there wasn't any softness in his expression. He was there to fight for his career, and part of me admired that. I'd seen models at the end of their career clawing and fighting to stay in the job.; I'd let them down as compassionately as I could. I'd held some of them as they cried, but at least they listened to me. I knew my business, and I knew when things needed to end.

But you don't know hockey.

I'd never seen anyone so focused and sure that he was

going to beat me. People didn't confront me. They wheedled and whined, and those weren't the models I ran; that was my management staff. All except Lucas, of course, who was the sole guy in charge of Gilded Treasures for the next week. There was some similarity between my business manager and the new coach. They were both self-assured, both had forceful personalities, but where Lucas was short and stout, Rowen was a big guy all solid muscle. Impressively solid. Confident.

I will not let him get in my head. I am stronger than an unwanted attraction to the man with the hazel eyes and the nerve to tell me what to do.

"He's a good-looking guy," Leigh said.

"He's taken the Mustangs far," Jason pointed out.

"And it's an impressive résumé," Leigh added and shuffled some papers.

Cameron whistled. "He was drafted first round, thirteenth overall by Montreal. He opted not to go play professionally and finished his time in college at the University of Western Ontario with a degree in, now get this, film studies. When he was called up for the big leagues, he discovered he was a hemophiliac, so he had to retire from the sport. He then went into coaching and began working his way up until he reached the pros via the Raptors."

I didn't know half of the words they used. I had an idea that the Frozen Four was some kind of college championship, but that was only because of the incident.

I pulled that particular article out. "See what he did?"

I'd seen a lot of photos of him, even zoomed in to look at the color of his eyes and the way his hair was styled just so, and the neatness of his beard. But in this one, he wore a cheap suit, the tie askew as in most of the photos he was gesturing at players from his place behind the bench. The article was labeled "2013 Frozen Four meltdown" in which our new coach was being escorted from the bench. The bench being where the skaters sat, or so I'd found out last night. Then I'd followed links to various sources for more about the incident and saw our coach Carmichael had gone head to head with referees and had done enough verbal damage to get himself kicked out of the game.

What kind of coach got himself dismissed from a game? *One that was out of control.*

I massaged my temples and waited for them to see what I'd found and back me up on finding a way to get this man away from our team.

"We need to get a coach from one of the original six teams," I said and hoped I sounded as if I knew what I was talking about. I didn't, but I knew that the original six teams likely had good coaches, right? "Or someone from one of the top teams in the NHL, someone who knows hockey."

"Seems to me this guy knows hockey," Jason said.

"How the hell would you know that?" I snapped. "Like you were anywhere near involved with Dad's stupid investment."

Jason straightened, shook his head. "You've been gone a long time, Mark. I've been here, along with Cameron, and we've kept this family afloat, even if you weren't—"

"Oh, wait, big brother, is this you changing the subject to comment on me not being here. Did you forget it was you who helped me pack my fucking bags to throw me out?"

Jason winced. "I wanted to—"

"Leave it." I'm not sure I knew what I was stopping him from saying. This conversation was less about hockey and more about my place in this messed-up family, and I wasn't ready for that.

"I know enough about hockey," Cameron murmured. "I mean, I didn't, but when Dad called me a month or two back to help him, I came home."

"Me too," Jason said.

The knife went deep into my chest. The old man hadn't called me. Not ten years ago, not two months ago, not the day he was taken ill and died. No, he'd just dumped my name into this convoluted shit of a will. I wasn't going to let Cam and Jason see my pain, and covered it with anger.

"And you both think this coach is what is best for the Raptors?" I used my best disbelieving tone.

My brothers glanced at each other and then looked at Leigh.

"Rowen Carmichael, assistant coach in the American college leagues for two seasons, moving to head coach in the U Sports level four years ago, winning Cavendish Farms University Cup twice. He's well known for his thoughtfulness and support for his players. His playing career suggests that adversity only makes him better, discipline is his main focus, which has earned his former team back-to-back wins against some of the bigger and better-funded teams. He took the Jean-Marie de Koninck Coaching Excellence Award twice, and in most reports, he's described as very detail-oriented."

I blinked at my sister. "Did you memorize that?"

She shook her head. "Whatever, Mark. Dad might not think much of the girl in the wheelchair, but don't you start thinking I'm stupid."

"No one said you were stupid," Jason said and leaned down to hug her. She accepted the hug and then pushed him away with a wrinkled nose.

"No pity." She smirked, and Jason smiled at her. They were brother and sister for real, and that hurt as well.

Again, I felt like I was on the edge of this family. Hell, so close to the edge I might just tip over completely.

"You should have the third of this mess he gave me," I said and scrubbed at my eyes. "He didn't want me, and I don't fucking want what he gave me."

Something hit my shin, hard, and I cursed, then as I realized Leigh had rolled her chair into me. I caught her expression, which was past angry and onto furious.

"Fuck off with the self-pity," she snapped.

"I'm not… it's not—"

She held up a hand, and I stopped talking.

"Dad threw you out to live in his idea of what Sodom and Gomorrah was, and he said you would burn in hell, yet you still get a third of his estate. So when it comes to self-pity, I get priority here, okay?"

"Okay," I mumbled. She was right. "But we should do something about this." I looked at Jason and Cameron. "Leigh deserves more."

Jason let out a full-body sigh. "We can't now. We tried. But Cam and I have already filed papers that are in force as soon as the year is up on these ridiculous terms Dad set. Splitting our portion with her."

"You did?" The brothers I remembered were stupid idiots who would rather tease Leigh than love her. Of course they were the same brothers fighting for Dad's affection and approval, which meant rubbing my face into the dirt more times than I wanted to recall. Anything to make me more of a man in Dad's eyes.

Now it was Cam's turn to twist the knife. "And we realize that would give you a controlling interest."

"I don't want a controlling interest. Fuck that. Hell, I don't want anything to do with this team or Dad's legacy or anything to do with the twisted bitter asshole." I pulled my shoulders back. "After the year is done, I'll give my share to Leigh. Then no one needs to worry about who owns what."

"So you're staying for the year?

"I didn't say that," I hedged.

"The will states you have to work for the two hundred days. Otherwise the entire concern is sold and split up to charities."

"And you'd personally lose millions. Blah, blah, I get that."

Jason shoved me.

If it had been Cameron, I would have shoved back, but the eldest of the three boys didn't shove people, and I was shocked into silence.

"None of us need the money, you idiot," he snapped. "We all have trust funds, even you if you decided not to touch it. But this team isn't just about us. It's about corporate partnerships and a thousand employees from managers to cleaners, players to administrators. For all its faults, the Raptors support several local charities, as well as youth teams, a sled team, educational outreach, and that is just the tip of the iceberg. Everything is failing, and we have a year to turn it around before those thousand people lose everything. Do you understand what I'm saying?"

He was poking at my chest, and I pushed his hand away. I knew all about a company supporting more than just the people who worked for it. Gilded Treasures partnered with five local LGBT shelters and worked with schools and the local colleges. Without the agency there might not be the representation and resources for at-risk teens that we provided.

"First thing then, I don't want Dad's money, so we liquidate my trust fund and dump it as an investment in the team. That way you can't hold that money shit over my head."

Then before they could say anything remotely angry, critical, or even kind and approving, I left.

———

I MEANT to go back to the hotel room I was staying in, but when it came to leaving the mansion, I typed in the zip code for the arena and headed there instead. All I could think of when I first saw it was that it was one hell of an expanse of glass.

A glass building in the Arizona sun.

The reflection was glaring, but I guessed that was to make some kind of design statement. I couldn't avoid knowing I'd arrived when I was temporarily blinded as I drew up to a barrier with Staff Only emblazoned on it. The security guard ambled out, looked sharply at my car, and leaned down to the window.

"Can I help you, sir?" he asked with suspicion.

"My name is Mark Westman-Reid, one of the owners here now."

He didn't believe me immediately; I could see that. "Can I see some ID, sir?"

"Here you go." I passed over my ID. He checked the picture against me and then nodded.

"I'll call ahead and let them know to expect you."

"No, don't do that. I'm here unofficially."

He tipped his hat and went back into his hut. "Have a nice day, sir."

"And you."

I parked next to a pale blue Mercedes S-Class and then messed around a bit longer to get my car as close to the wall on the passenger side as possible. I loved my car. She wasn't the most expensive Lamborghini out there, but she was all mine. Not only that, but she'd carried me all the way from New York to here for this apparently-I-own-a-hockey-team shitfest. I wanted to show her some respect. No dings in her doors on my watch.

I heard a low whistle of appreciation and turned to see a young guy who couldn't have been more than twenty or so, dressed in Raptors colors and carrying a bundle of sticks.

"Thank you."

"Murcielago? Four-wheel drive, V12, six-speed shift, zero to sixty-two 3.8, top speed over two hundred, right?"

"Yeah."

"My dad's new husband or my stepdad or whatever"—he rolled his eyes dramatically—"he wanted one of these. But he wants to get it resprayed to Railers' blue, not the red." He thrust out his hand. "Ryker Madsen."

The name was on the list of skaters I'd memorized. Ryker Madsen, one of the team's rookies.

"Mark," I said and conveniently left off the incriminating Westman-Reid.

"You going in?" He inclined his head toward the arena back entrance, and I nodded. He kept up a long, chattering monologue about the Arizona weather, *hot as balls*, the team, *not bad*, and cars, *my boyfriend wants a jeep.*

The mention of a boyfriend hit me. I hadn't realized that being gay in hockey was a thing. I'd clearly missed a memo. Or maybe this kid just didn't understand the toxic world of being gay in sports or business and how it was best not to own the fact unless it was to your benefit.

Luckily, being the owner of a modeling agency meant I could be as gay as I damn well wanted.

We passed through more security, but Ryker was babbling about hockey sticks and didn't pay any attention to the wide-eyed look I received from the security guy.

"Okay, bye," he said and took a left down a narrow

corridor. I carried on ahead, not sure where I was going or why I was doing it but then took the next left. This led me to a storage room, a medical space, and then on to offices with shut doors. I didn't like the shut door policy, and it wasn't something that happened at my company— something else for me to bring up whenever we had a meeting. The last door on the right was ajar, and I stood outside, reading the sign next to the door. It was held up with sticky tape and gave a very simple message. *If you're bleeding, then medical is back the way you came. If you want to whine, then I'm not in.*

The nameplate was blank, but I had a hunch this was Coach Carmichael's office. I knocked, but it was empty, so I carried on and ended up finding a door to the ice and a row of seats where I sat and watched.

Nobody was out on the ice yet, and the air was cool and smelled like air conditioning. I sat patiently, and finally one by one, the players in red-and-white jerseys skated out onto the ice. There was some pushing and shoving, but I couldn't tell if it was good-natured or not, and then he came out—Coach Carmichael.

He spoke to the group, who all took a knee in front of him, and then there was some exchanging of jerseys, which I guessed split the team into two practice sides. He set them off sprinting from one end to the other, and then he smoothly skated toward me. Perhaps not actually toward *me*, just in my general direction.

And then he stopped.

From the other side of the plexiglass, he skated to a halt, and leaning on his stick, he stared right at me. I didn't know where to look, but I couldn't glance away. I was mesmerized, hot under the collar, and he kept staring. I waited for him to say something or shout through the glass or give me the bird or *something*.

But no, he just studied me as if he had nothing better to do.

I wriggled in my chair a little, but I still couldn't take my eyes off him. He was in a Raptors jacket, gloves on his hands, but unlike the team he was working with, he wasn't wearing a helmet, which meant I got a good look at his perfectly styled hair. A whistle hung around his neck, and when I tracked my gaze downward as far as I could see and then up past his lips and caught his gaze again, he lifted an eyebrow in silent communication.

Shit. Busted.

With a nod, he left and headed back to doing whatever coaches do.

Was it possible that someone staring at me through plexiglass could qualify as one of the most sensual experiences of my life?

All I could say was from the evidence of my erection to the rapid beating of my heart, it would seem that yes, Coach Carmichael staring at me was definitely on my top ten list of erotic moments.

Shit.

FOUR

Rowen

THERE WERE a thousand and one things I needed to do before I left the rink. None of them were to sit in my office, reflecting on how incredibly hot Mark Westman-Reid had been when our eyes had met and held. He'd been more than a little turned on. That was obvious from the way his pupils had swallowed the sweet milk chocolate brown of his eyes. The man had been pretty blatant in his appreciation of my body, which only added to the slow fattening of my cock that had been taking place over the past few minutes. Shifting a bit to alleviate the pressure of my pants riding a raging erection, I shoved the pages of player profiles and training reports to the side and did a quick Google search of the princeling.

Yes, that title seemed to fit the gorgeous but prickly man I'd been mentally undressing. The Internet loved Mark Westman-Reid—that much was obvious. His business acumen, his stance on LGBT rights, his proud life as an out gay man and a philanthropist who donated and hosted charity galas for a New York children's hospice, a large animal shelter, and to forward the discussion of wind energy. All noble causes. I donated anonymously to the wind energy coalition he backed as well. While Mark was vocal about his gayness, I'd not thrown the closet door open as he had. When I'd come into the game, people didn't talk about gays, and you certainly didn't come out as openly as Tennant Rowe had. I admired that about Rowe and even about Mark. I'd been happy enough dating men discreetly over the years, but perhaps it was time to contemplate making a formal announcement of some kind...

"Thoughts for another day," I whispered, leaping from one website to another, checking out the online images of Westie, as his chic Manhattan friends seemed to call him. Princeling fit the smug bastard much better if you asked me. Westie seemed a name a hockey player would carry. Mark was as far from a hockey player as I was from a Manhattan fashion model.

Four rapid sharp knocks on the door brought my gaze off the Internet. I cleared the search page and brought up the player profiles I'd supposedly been working on, before beckoning whoever was out to come in. Mark stepped through the door. My eyes flared in surprise. He stopped right in front of my desk, his big brown eyes resting on me. Lord, but he was a pretty, pretty man.

"I'd like to discuss this trip to find an associate coach," he stated.

I leaned back in my chair, folded my arms over my favorite worn white dress shirt, and cocked an eyebrow. He cocked right back. Sassy little brat. Something about the little shit was wiggling under my flesh. It felt like a thorn. A princely irritant that would need to be dug out with my jackknife.

"We can discuss it over dinner," my mouth said. My brain skidded to a halt as it wondered when and how the cock-to-mouth connection had been established. Also, why? He drew back as if he'd been presented with a severed head. "It's a barbecue at my place with the rookies. Perhaps you could actually spend time with your team, get to know the players a little? It might make you less... what's the word I'm looking for? Clenched? No. Strained? Mm, no. Priggish? Well, that one fits as well, but it's not quite the proper term. Bossy?"

He placed both hands onto the top of my desk. One side of my mouth twitched. No twitching of his mouth took place.

"I *am* your boss," he reminded me flatly. "So, if I'm acting bossy, that means I'm doing my job."

I shrugged. He looked flustered. Good. Little heirs needed to be reminded that the world didn't revolve around them, even if they did have kissable mouths and curls that needed to be finger-combing and tugged while someone was fucking them from behind.

Rowen, what in the name of fuck are you doing inviting this haughty brat to come to your place? Have you lost all your marbles? The kids won't want one of the owners there. Oh, okay, we're thinking with our dick now. Wonderful. Just great. Hey, moron! Does the name Carl ring a bell?

"... rookie dinner I'd be happy to come over and meet them. Maybe we can discuss this associate coach business in more detail. Time and place?"

"Six p.m. my place."

"Good." He stood up and walked to the door, giving me a fine view of a high, tight ass covered with cool tan linen material. The man could dress, there was no faulting him there, and obviously his summer trousers had been expertly fitted, as they hugged his buttocks just perfectly. Out he went, never glancing back. The door closed. I waited. Ten seconds later, the door creaked open, and Mark strode back into my office. "I'll need your address."

"Main office has it. The Raptors are paying for my accommodations until I find a permanent address, also one of the addendums to my contract— to save you time with that fine-toothed comb I'm sure you're going over my paperwork with."

He wanted to say something badly. There was even a slight curling of his upper lip that took place. I waited patiently as he found the words.

"You're insufferable," he informed me before spinning around and exiting with all the flair only a New York model could muster. Would clapping be the right thing to do here? Would he come storming back in, eyes fiery, nostrils flared, sensuous mouth set, and call me another stuffy name? God, that would be kind of exciting. My cock sure thought so. And that was a whole different kettle of very dangerous fish. Piranha chowder to be precise. And me without any oyster crackers.

HE ARRIVED at ten after six. Fashionably late he would call it. I called it fucking rude.

I flung the door open, and Mark blinked at me in shock after my front door barely missed his snobby nose.

"I said be here at six."

He peeked around me, then thrust a bottle of wine at me as his gaze returned to my face. "No one else is here yet," he pointed out casually.

"That's because they're coming at seven. I told you to be here at six. You do realize that being late is highly unmannerly?"

He breezed around me and entered my place as if he

owned it. Which he kind of did, but that wasn't the point at all here. I closed the door with a bit of vigor.

"I got bound up in some multitasking. Trust me, Coach Carmichael, I wasn't trying to get your panties in a twist. I'm now running two businesses on separate coasts. Time simply got away from me."

"Being late is inconsiderate and shows that you are incapable of managing your time efficiently. Also, it's a selfish behavioral trait that I won't brook. If you're not on time to meet the plane on Friday, I will instruct them to take off without you."

I stomped into the kitchen to shove the wine into the refrigerator.

"Don't refrigerate that. It's a petite sirah and should be served at room temperature," the princeling called. I jerked the door of the fridge open and yanked the damn wine out, then set it soundly on the counter. "I wasn't sure what you were serving and thought a light red would go with most anything."

I returned to the living room, stopping dead, a bitter retort on my tongue, to find Mark reading over my vast collection of CDs. He'd toned down his clothes a bit. Now he was in a blue shirt with the sleeves casually rolled to his elbows, white slacks that showed a good deal of his ankles, and black suede loafers with small silver buckles. A chunky silver watch sat on his left wrist, and his hair was windblown. The man was far too attractive. Maybe if I just took a deep breath and let it out through one nostril I could—

"I haven't seen one of these in years." He plucked one of my CDs out of the wooden case that housed them, a taunting smirk playing on his lips. "I think my grandmother has some stored with her 8-tracks and bell-bottom pants. Hmm, The Eagles. Never heard of them. Are any of them still alive?"

"Didn't any of your deportment teachers tell you that it's rude to come into someone's home and make fun of their personal items?" I stalked over and took the CD from him, the smell of his cologne tickling my nose. "And yes, quite a few of them are still alive." I placed *Hotel California* back in place in chronological order by date released.

"Probably need walkers to get on stage." He bent down to study my movie collection, his nose wrinkling more and more tightly as he looked over the fantasy films. "So you like dragons and elves and knightly things? That's... interesting. I prefer more socially significant films, you know, the kinds that rely on acting and not Harry riding CGI hippogriffs."

"I have to turn the potatoes," I told him, leaving him to sneer alone. Snotty self-absorbed asshole—curls and plunderable mouth aside. The grill sat on my small patio, shaded nicely, a gleaming beauty with a side burner and room for all the baking potatoes that were already on the heat. As I rolled the foil-wrapped spuds, something came to me. I closed the lid and walked back inside. Mark was resting on my sofa, scrolling through his phone. His gaze darted to me when I entered, the look a curious one.

"You knew Harry rode a hippogriff." I walked past him into the kitchen, feeling rather proud of myself.

He entered on my heels. "I saw the trailer," Mark quickly informed me.

I gave him a nod and a yeah-sure kind of look, then started pulling out salad fixings. "Do you know how to make a salad or did the staff prepare all of your meals?"

He bristled up like a bantam rooster. I was growing quite fond of that look and the high color it brought to his cheeks.

"I know how to cut a damn cucumber," he snapped, so I gave him a long, fat cuke and the cutting board. "You seem to think I had this fairy-tale life, but I've sat huddled on heat grates in New York City, so you can just stop poking at me for being an elitist."

That brought me up short. Perhaps I should have read more about his life instead of gawking at his IG images from Portugal or Miami as he lounged around in swim trunks and a glowing tan.

"Sorry, I didn't realize," I said as sincerely as I could.

He gave me a curt nod, washed his hands in the big double sink, and then started chopping the cucumber. Bits of dark green skin flew all over the counter, but I didn't mention it. I focused on my task.

"Tell me about this associate coach you want to talk to," he said, after a moment of stilted silence engulfed us.

"I'd rather hold off until you meet them. It will keep you from jumping to conclusions as you did about me being a lowly college coach," I said, cutting the fat tomato into chunks on my own small board. "We can discuss the lack of quality goalkeeping the team has and the dismal prospects in the pipeline."

"Uhm, okay." I glanced over. He was intent on his cucumber slicing. "I'm not sure exactly what you expect me to say."

"Well, for starters, you could say that your father and the old guard understood jack shit about drafting well. Aside from a few key kids who were picked up here and there, Ryker Madsen being one, your rebuild is going to take years. It will anyway, but you need to unload the deadwood on this team and bring in new talent. I have some suggestions."

I waved my knife at the list hanging on the fridge.

"Wonderful. He made a list." I heard him mutter and

smiled to myself. "Of course I'll look over your suggestions and present them to my siblings. We'll be taking a more hands-on approach now that we understand some of the poor decisions Dad made." Our eyes met. "Hiring you not one of those poor decisions, I'm sure."

"Mm-hmm."

A few minutes went past with the sound of chopping and slicing filling the cool air.

"This goaltending situation," he said, when I passed over a red onion for him to peel and slice. "If you had any say, which you do not as player choice is not part of your coaching staff hiring caveat, but *if* you had any say, whom would you go after?"

"You'll see on the way back from Seattle. We're dropping into Nevada before we come home, to talk to him. We could touch on what we need to do with Aarni Lankinen."

His lips settled into a fine line. "I'm not at liberty to discuss players' contracts with you. But we are aware of his past indiscretions and are hoping to sit down with him and make him an offer."

"Look, I know he has a no-move clause. It's public knowledge."

"It is?"

"Yes, anyone can look up the team and what the players' contracts are. I also know that your father and his advisors made a mistake signing him. He's a cancer. His history is full of cheap shots that have severely maimed and injured other players. If you and your siblings are serious about making this team into something, then he has to go. The tension he stirs up in the locker room is palpable."

"Thank you for your input. We're currently in discussions on how to handle this situation," he replied tersely.

My mouth opened. The doorbell rang. I let the Aarni situation drop. I could see he was tense—his jaw was set and his shoulders tight. I wiped my hands on my jeans, walked over to him, and placed my hand on the back of his neck. His head flew up and spun to face me, eyes wide, lips soft and parted.

There was a split second of free fall. My eyes fell to his mouth. He wet his lips. All it would take would be for me to lead his mouth to mine with a gentle bit of guidance from my fingers biting into his neck. The doorbell rang again. The ghost of Carl, the angelic egomaniac from long ago, reappeared and slapped me silly. I pulled my hand from his neck.

"Good then. Good." Then I hustled off to the front door, glancing back once or twice as I chided myself for even *thinking* of kissing the man. He was *so* not my type. It would be a massive mistake on so many levels. Also, we disliked each other. Deeply. Must have been a hormone surge brought on by a lengthy dick drought.

Shaking off the moment of insanity, I opened the door. Five young men stood there, all smiling nervously at me.

"You're all early," I said, then gave them a welcoming smile. "Welcome to Casa Carmichael. Come in. Hey, Ryker," I said, offering Jared Madsen's boy my hand. This one had potential. As did the next fellow through the door, Alejandro Garcia, or Alex as he was known in the dressing room. "Alex, welcome. Come in." Tim, Drake, and Josh also filed in, each looking as tense as the others. "We're outside. Just step through that way. I'll get the steaks, and we'll eat soon."

The guys headed outside. Mark met me at the doorway, a massive bowl of salad in his hands. He sidled around me, eyes on his bowl of greens, and slipped outside before I could say anything. Probably for the best if I were being honest. Shoving the free fall into his eyes aside, I went into the kitchen and pulled out the covered platter of fat steaks, and carried them to the grill. The guys were standing around my cactus, a twenty-foot saguaro beauty, whom I'd named Spikes McGhee, staring at the white cowboy hat with the shiny gold star I'd tossed up onto the crown of the cactus.

"Uhm, Coach," Ryker began, "Is there a reason there's a hat on this cactus?"

"That's Spikes McGhee, and he's sheriff around these parts."

"Dear God, he named a cactus," Mark muttered, then crouched by the cooler to get a drink. The guys gathered around Spikes McGhee chuckled, and the tension lessened a bit. Mark pawed through the cans of Dr Pepper for several minutes. "Isn't there anything besides Dr Pepper in here?"

"Nope. There *is* nothing but Dr Pepper. Dr Pepper *is* life." I gave the kids a wink, then began dropping the rested steaks onto the grill, the hiss and smoke making my stomach rumble in anticipation.

Mark huffed and puffed and ended up drinking wine. Within thirty minutes, we were all at my new picnic table, eating rare steak and buttered baked potatoes with huge sides of salad. *On the Border* was playing inside, the beautiful early songs of the Eagles drifting outside. Mark and the rookies had all relaxed by now, which was a good thing. The uppity-ups had to get to know the players, especially these new ones, if they wanted to build a dynasty on their broad young backs.

"The thing I want you all to know is this." I wiped my face with my napkin, then met all the expectant looks. "I am going to work you hard. Make no mistake. But I will always be fair, and I will always be willing to talk to you." I glanced at Ryker, then at Alex. Mark was chewing a bite of steak as I spoke. He'd been quiet as we'd talked about our love of hockey, who our idols were, and when we'd known this sport would be our life. Obviously, he'd felt left out, but that was okay. He could stand to sit and listen to the rookies on his team. "I will ask you to learn my system, but I will never take your creativity away from you. I'm just going to ask you to work hard, learn, and grow. And above all, enjoy yourselves because if you *do* make the team, you will remember your rookie season as long as you live, and I want you all to smile when you recall it."

Grins and nods followed. I clapped Ryker on the shoulder and then told him about my one and only time playing against his father. When the tale was done, the guys were all laughing and swapping stories about other great defensemen. Mark's gaze and mine met over the platter that now held the T-shaped bones from our meal. Spikes towered behind him; the setting sun warmed his skin and eyes. It had to be the sunset making his gaze so tender. Right?

FIVE

Mark

_____

I GOT AWAY from the barbecue before Rowen could corner me again. I'd spent most of the time in the backyard, wondering what the hell had just happened in the kitchen and trying not to look at him. Stupid-ass cactus with the name and all that Dr Pepper, but I refused to find any of it remotely cute. Because I swear he'd meant to kiss me, and that fact alone was fucking terrifying. I almost made it out to the safety of my car when he caught me.

"You leaving?" he asked from his front door. I glanced up to see him leaning on the frame, his muscled arms crossed over his chest, looking all kinds of sexy.

"Yes." I kept my cool and refused to go into any long-winded explanation of why I was leaving or how unsettled I felt. I had things I needed to do, and first on the list was calling my brothers and actually doing what I'd told Rowen I'd already done, which was discussing contracts and Aarni Lankinen.

"You want to drive to the airport after practice on Saturday, or would you rather ride with me?"

The thought of sitting in a car with Rowen for any

length of time was vaguely horrifying. I'd barely managed to avoid going over and dry humping him in the yard, let alone having to handle being in close proximity to him. *You're going to be in a plane with him on Saturday, idiot.*

Why was I having such a strong reaction to him? He was snarky, irreverent, a freaking idiot, and the wrong person for this team, but somehow he'd gotten under my skin. I didn't like it, and I didn't want it. I liked to do things alone, and he was messing with my mojo.

I'd been on my own in business since the day I was pulled from the street to model. Some might call that a fairy-tale ending. I called it dumb fucking luck that I was begging for money outside the right coffee shop at the right time on only the tenth day of sleeping in doorways.

Alone was a state of mind that I craved, and solitary didn't have to mean lonely. I had friends; Lucas, my business manager, was as close as a brother—closer actually, given my brothers had washed their hands of me. In fact, I'd learned early on not to depend on anyone. And it wasn't just because of my family. The modeling industry hated me as well. They didn't take kindly to a messed-up kid saving his money and doing his own thing and on his way through going against the norm. They'd seen me as nothing more than a body that sold magazines, and most of them hated that I wanted to be more. Or at least it had felt that way. I'd scraped and wheedled and forced my way up, wanting more than just being a pretty face. I wanted respect, and I worked damned hard to get it.

Rowen doesn't respect me. Rowen is just another asshole for me to fight.

"I'll meet you there. I have business to attend to," I lied and winced internally. I sounded like an idiot, and from his smirk, he didn't believe me anyway.

"Okay, then," he said, then waved and went back into

the house. I had never climbed into my car as fast as I did then. I slipped and slid on the leather seat, got tangled in the seat belt, got my jacket hooked on the door, and finally in frustration, I had to take a minute to calm the hell down. I didn't need know-it-all coaches riding my ass or making me feel I was being laughed at.

Nope. I needed a beer and my laptop to catch up on work.

And maybe a shower where I got myself off to images of the infuriating coach on his knees sucking me dry.

Oh, fuck my life. Now I'm hard, and my cock is trapped in my pants.

WE'D MANAGED to get a nonstop flight to Seattle. Or at least Miriam in the back office had. That meant our flying time was only three hours or so, but that didn't account for the time at Tucson International or the waiting on the tarmac for takeoff. Luckily Rowen kept himself to himself, thumbing through a thick notebook filled with unintelligible scribble. I know it was indecipherable because I'd tried to read it with sideways glances. Part of me hoped that it would give me an insight into Rowen, something I could hold onto in order to regain equilibrium, but all I could see were Xs and Os and arrows. From the way they were laid out, I finally assumed they were game plans. I bet coaches at better teams than ours would've loved to get their hands on his book to see if there was anything in there that was worth a look.

I doubt it, though, given his coaching level was so far below what most pro teams would consider.

The flight wasn't full, and we were lucky enough that there was just the two of us in the final few rows. He took a window seat, put in earbuds, pulled a cap over his eyes, and leaned to one side, his head pillowed by his jacket.

Then he went to sleep. Just like that, without mentioning that he was going to sleep or even a smile or gesture of apology.

What if I'd wanted to talk hockey? *I don't want to talk hockey. I don't even like hockey.*

From my seat across the aisle, I reached over and poked him when they did the safety talk. He grunted, opened his eyes, gave attention to what the flight attendant said, and immediately resumed his sleep position.

I've never been able to sleep on commercial flights, even when I had the room to stretch out. There used to be a time when the Westman-Reid family had a private jet, and I'd loved using that, with the unlimited snacks and the TV screens. But the jet was long gone, an indulgence that hadn't been used enough to justify it. I'd seen the Raptors with their own jet, but apparently that was one of the first things to go three years ago, and now the team used a charter flight whose cost they shared with various other teams in different seasons.

Because of the non-sleeping, I buried myself in work instead, answering all the emails I'd had concerning Gilded Treasures, and then passing on what I could to Lucas. He'd already cleared most of the issues, and if I was completely honest with myself, I'd reached a point where I didn't even need to be in the office full-time. The team I'd built was honest, strong, and everything worked like clockwork. I was the first to admit that I'd been edgy for a while now and had even looked at starting up something new, just to get that buzz of winning. Only I never imagined that my new start would be working with Jason, Cameron, and Leigh.

I pulled up the contract my dad and Rowen Carmichael had signed. I wasn't a lawyer or an expert in anything legal at all, but on the surface, I couldn't see a way of getting out of it. There was no clause talking about an early release payment or anything like that. His salary was fixed, his signature strong, and it looked as if we were stuck with him. I just hoped that my dad's last act wasn't going to ruin everything.

Wait. Something jumped out at me.

I reread the contract. There was a clause I'd read, something about thirty-five points, and I skimmed until I reached it. The Raptors had to be showing a minimum of thirty-five points by midseason at the end of January; otherwise clause seven would be enacted. I scrolled up to the clause in question, and there it was in black and white. If the Raptors didn't get the magic thirty-five by January 31st, then the owners of the team, being the three Westman-Reid siblings—poor Leigh—could revoke the contract.

I worked my way through the process. The season started in October, and if we couldn't get rid of him until the end of January, then that was a long time to have to put up with someone who might not be a good fit for the job. I researched a bit more and saw that historically, over the past ten years or so, the *better* NHL teams had fifty points or more at the halfway point.

Again, all I could think was that we needed an excellent coach, someone who would pull this team up by its bootstraps. I doubted we had that in some college guy who might have once played hockey for a big team. Particularly one who had the perfect opportunity to discuss the future with me and had decided to go to sleep instead.

With at least another two hours to kill, I pulled up YouTube and searched on the word "hockey." Then expanded it to "what is hockey." The first video I found was "How to play hockey—basic hockey rules explained."

I followed the video, mumbling as I watched in order to try and recall what I was listening to. Then I clicked on more links and watched actual game footage. "Three periods," I murmured.

A hand on my shoulder had me shooting up in my chair and nearly cracking my head on the overhead bins. I turned to face a smirking Rowen staring down at me.

"That's not what you want to watch," he said and held out his hand for my iPad.

"Sorry?"

He waggled his hand a little, and reluctantly I passed him the tablet. He sat in the seat next to me, and abruptly he was up close and personal. This near, I could see how neat his beard was, and wondered idly how long it took him to get himself looking as good as he did. He wasn't model-perfect, there was a scar by his right eye and laughter lines bracketed his eyes, but his skin seemed soft, and his lips were pouty and kissable. I could appreciate that he was a fine-looking specimen, as men go, and he didn't really look his age, although what I was expecting a forty-one-year-old to look like, I didn't know. I guessed I expected him to be more hockey-worn because to me it seemed hockey players were Neanderthals who beat each other up for a living. I'd spent half an hour down the rabbit hole of watching hockey fights, and some of them were brutal. Maybe that was how he got the scar? Not that I would ask him because that meant he'd know I'd been checking him out.

"This." With a few taps, he pulled up footage from a game between Chicago and New York, and as the game progressed, he explained one or two things, like the fact that shoving the goalie was a bad thing but slamming someone into the boards was good, unless it was by smacking them *in the numbers,* which was the term for the big numbers they all wore on their backs right under their names in jock-lettering.

"I can pull up specific plays. Are you a fan of a team?" he asked as if the answer wasn't important at all.

"New York," I lied immediately. New York had a team, and he'd just shown me them. After all, I'd walked past Madison Square Garden often enough to have seen the huge pictures there of some of the sexiest men I'd ever seen all in red, white, and blue.

"Their rebuild looks good," Rowen commented and settled back in the seat next to me, and I thought he was going back to sleep. I didn't want that. I wanted to get to know him, dig inside his head, and work out if the team and everyone it supported was fucked. But I wanted to do it without him thinking I was remotely interested.

I'm so messed up.

"A new arena?" I asked. Anything to get him talking.

"No, a rebuild is when a team takes a year to work out kinks. This is what the Raptors are doing this year."

"I knew that," I defended.

All he did was chuckle. "No, you didn't."

Ass.

BY THE TIME we were in the cab leaving SeaTac, I'd watched a lot of YouTube videos. Some of it had sunk in; some of them were incredibly exciting, not that I would tell Rowen that, because then he would've gotten smug again.

"Tell me more about the associate coach we're meeting."

"Hiring," he corrected.

I gave him the patented pissed-off-Mark face, which always had my employees back in New York scrambling to agree with me. Only he just sat there waiting for me to correct his correction and call me contrary, but I wasn't going to give him the satisfaction.

"Anderson, thirty-four, skating coach with Anaheim, Calgary, became the director of skating development at the Athletes Training Center with Buffalo, and is currently a development manager at the Seattle Thunder AHL team."

"So he knows his way around a rink?"

He glanced at me then, and I swear he was going to say something, but instead he looked back out the window as we passed over the bridge and took a left, following a sign for the SeaTac arena. It was kind of rude, but I'd had worse. My phone vibrated with a message, and I thumbed it open as soon as I saw it was from Cameron. He was the one tasked with looking into the Aarni situation, and I hoped he would have some news for us. My heart sank when I read the message. Aarni's contract was solid, and unless we could convince him to waive the no-move contract he'd signed, then we were stuck with him. Aarni had definitely not been on Rowen's list on his fridge. I knew that because I'd memorized all the names. Then I'd pulled them all up and fallen into the mess that was contract negotiations and trade deals. Every article I read about the Raptors said that Aarni was poisonous, but he'd put up an impressive amount of points last year or at least got above the average for defensemen in the NHL. Although why a defenseman would be scoring goals, I couldn't work out.

The article that stood out was the one reporting the incident between Aarni and Tennant Rowe, and there was a lot of heated debate about that issue, which had rumbled on for weeks. Tennant, a superstar forward, was on Rowen's list under a heading of *yeah, right*, along with a couple of other high-powered names. I did check into

Tennant's contract details as much as I could, but he was staying. On the other hand, rumors were abound that another superstar forward, Tate Collins, was pissed with his team right now, and maybe I should discuss this with Rowen. Maybe make a deal or a trade or whatever it's called.

I loved making deals. The rush of it was intoxicating, and the Raptors needed something amazing. We had the new kids, but we needed star power as well.

The arena we stopped at wasn't as fancy as the Raptors', but then this team we were visiting was in something called the AHL, which was the level below NHL and was the development level for the big leagues.

I guessed it was a step up from college hockey, although I didn't say that.

There was a woman in sweats and a Seattle Thunder jacket waiting for us, and she approached us with hand extended, which I shook.

"Mark Westman-Reid and Rowen Carmichael for Terri Anderson," I announced.

She smiled at me. Classically pretty, she had clear blue eyes, and her fine blonde hair was twisted into a messy bun. I wasn't interested in women at all, but if I'd have been doing some sort of shoot for a health magazine, I would've chosen her.

"Terri? You've found her," she said with a laugh and released my hand to shake Rowen's.

Wait, what? Terri Anderson was a *woman*? I knew for damn sure that NHL hockey was a man's game, right? I was all for equality, but this wasn't what I'd expected at all.

"Can I have a private word, Rowen?" I asked and inclined my head to indicate the door we'd just come through.

Terri faced me, but she was talking to Rowen. "You didn't tell him I was actually Teresa, then?"

Rowen shrugged as if he didn't care. "Gender isn't an issue. If you're what the team needs, then that is what I will pay for."

"Rowen—"

"We'd like to offer you a contract. One year, no probation, and the figures we agreed are detailed in here." He passed over an envelope, and she took it. "Can we go somewhere to discuss it?"

She led us into a room, closed the door, and then waited for us to sit before leaning against a table in the corner. The room was full of Seattle Thunder posters and memorabilia, and I realized we were in the team's archive area.

"When could you start?" Rowen asked.

"I haven't said I'll do it yet," Terri answered and slid a finger under the seal of the envelope, then pulled out a sheaf of papers.

"You're wasted here." Rowen leaned forward in his chair. "You and I together could do great things with the Raptors. I've been watching you for years, and your style is no-nonsense but compassionate. I need you to be there as my conscience, to show me when I might be too black and white. I'm headhunting you because you are exactly the right person for the job. Now all you need to do is say yes."

"We should talk about this," I interrupted, feeling as if I should make some kind of protest. After all, I was there to keep Rowen in check.

"Mr. Westman-Reid, did you read my contract?" Rowen asked.

"Yes, but—"

"Then you'll know that my choice stands."

I swear that if I'd been bigger, harder, and had

completed more than one lesson in Tae Kwan Do, I'd have been smacking that superior expression right off his face.

As it was, I had to suck it up and smile at our newest hire. But the minute we were out of there, the shit would be hitting the fan big-time.

He needed to be made *completely* aware of how he fitted into this management team, and *I* would be the one to show him.

SIX

Rowen

MARK WAS CHOMPING at the bit. It was kind of funny to watch him swallow down the tirade he'd been waiting to unleash upon me. Pity he'd not been able to vent his obviously swollen spleen due to Terri walking us to our car, grinning widely, even though she was still playing at being coy. She'd take the offer; I felt it in my bones. To be the first woman associate coach in the NHL would be a huge feather in her cap and would help promote the feminist ideals my mother had raised me with. Also, she was the most qualified person for the job, gender being a nonissue for me in terms of who served as my second. It would be for others, but that wasn't my problem. That was the problem of the owners and the PR department. Maybe they could hire the guy who handled the madness of the Tennant Rowe "I'm Gay and Dating my Coach!" announcement. Not my circus and not my monkey, as the saying goes.

Which brought us back to the youngest male heir, who had probably bitten his tongue in half by now. The ride from Terri's rink back to the airport found me and the

Uber driver chatting the entire way. Then the rush at the airport to catch our flight to Nevada barred him from unloading on me. Of course he had to be polite on the airplane and the small puddle jumper I'd arranged to take us from Reno-Tahoe International to the itsy-bitsy airport ten miles from Loveland, Nevada, population one thousand and nine hundred, according to the Internet.

Mark disembarked and did a complete one-eighty, his carry-on riding on his left shoulder. A hot wind tugged at his dark curls.

"There are only two runways," he said and looked at me to verify as his mind seemed to be stuck on that fact.

"All you need is one, right?" I tossed at him as I stalked past him and into the coolness of the small but nice airport. I could hear him mumbling, but whatever he was saying, he kept to himself. Picking up a rental car was easy, and in no time I was sitting in a lovely blue Pontiac Grand Prix, sipping on a Dr Pepper as Mark finally detonated.

"… contract may give you final decisions on who this team will employ. It does not give you the right to make up contracts! Furthermore, Terri is a woman. I'm all for breaking glass ceilings and all that, but—"

I lowered the bottle from my mouth, and our eyes met. "If you have to add 'but' to your statement, then you're really not for whatever it is you're claiming to be supporting."

He did a fine guppy-on-the-carpet imitation. I smiled and turned up the AC, hoping it would start blowing cool air soon.

"Okay, just fuck you. Fuck you all over the place! As a gay man who has lived his life facing down homophobia from the world and his own family, I am highly insulted by your casual assumption that I'm some sort of sexist pig!"

"Then stop sounding like one." I threw the car into reverse and backed out of our slot by the airport.

"You're an egotistical ass. You do know that, right?" I nodded and eased the Pontiac into drive, eager to be on the way. We had a long night ahead, trying to woo a player who might not want to be wooed, and this time, I didn't have a copy of a contract to dangle under anyone's nose. Player acquisition was fully on the owners and team management. "Just for your information, Coach, there are more women and people of color in upper management at Gilded Treasures than there are white male workers. I take pride in that. If you would have let me finish instead of charging in like a… a…"

"Bull?" I peeked over after we pulled up to the airport exit. He was in high pique, and it was truly a lovely sight. Cheeks pink and nostrils flared. The man was gorgeous when he was fired up. *Imagine what he would look like spread under you in bed, his skin flushed and his cock spewing cum as you plow him like a cornfield.*

Wow, okay. That was unexpectedly graphic but wholly arousing.

"Yes! Like a bull. You would have heard me say that while I'm all for breaking glass ceilings and all that, but this is going to be an uphill fight not only with the stockholders of the team but also upper management, the players, and the fans."

"Not my worry. I'm here to build a team, not play politics with your brothers and other rich assholes who worry about stock market dips." We wheeled out onto a two-lane road, my dick a little more at attention than it should be during a business discussion. "Your father hired me to clean up the Raptors because he saw it was dying. A fish rots from the head down, and when teams are in the dumpster, it's the coaching staff that goes first."

He stared at me for the longest time. "And certain players."

"Well, yes, and certain players but overall the head coach gets fired first."

"What is so damn special about one woman?"

"Look her up on YouTube. Search for the Vancouver Olympics women's ice hockey series and then find the final game between Team USA and Team Canada. Make sure you pay close attention to the young blonde woman with "Anderson" across her back. She'll be easy to find. She'll be the one scoring the hat trick that led her team to the gold medal. When you've done all that homework, then come back to me, and we'll talk about why Terri is the perfect person for the position."

He nodded, his lips flattened, which was a damn shame because they were so fat and nibble-worthy when he wasn't pressing them together. I plugged my phone into the stereo and filled the nicely cooling car with "Lyin' Eyes" from the *Take it to the Limit* album.

Those tempting lips of his puckered as if he'd just sucked off a lemon. "The Eagles?"

"That you even have to ask makes me sad for you."

The eye roll was epic and quite regal. I bit back a smile as we cruised closer to Loveland and the Silver Newt Lounge on the outskirts of town. When we pulled up to the two-bit saloon, Mark and I exchanged looks. There were a large number of Harleys parked outside the establishment. And not the cushy roadsters that most senior riders got on to travel around on. These were mean-looking bikes with riders to match, or so I assumed. The parking lot was full. So full there were cars and motorcycles and trucks parked up and down the long stretch of desert road as far as the eye could see.

"And we're going in here, why?" he asked, eying the

brick building with the flashing C ORS LIGH sign in the lone window like a tiger about to pounce.

"This is where we find Colorado," I said, turned off the engine, pocketed the keys, and exited the car. A small wind whipped across the dirt parking lot, the dust devil picking up gum wrappers and bits of dead leaves as it raced past our car and out over the road.

Mark got out of the car and met me at the door. "We find Colorado in Nevada?"

"That we do, my young prince." I clapped his shoulder and pushed into the biker bar, the first strains of a Metallica cover by the opening band so loud it nearly blew the door out of my hand. Mark balked. I took him by the wrist and shoved him into the standing room only audience. We threaded through the crowd until we managed to wade close to the bar. I held up two fingers and pointed at the Coors tap. The barkeep, a young woman with a pink Mohawk and several rings in her ears, nose, and eyebrows, nodded and poured us two mugs of cold beer.

"I don't like that beer," Mark shouted when I handed him his mug.

"Tough." I leaned into the bar. "When does Chaotic Furball come on?" I yelled as the opening band roared and raged onstage. I handed her a ten, then nodded when she held up five fingers. I nudged Mark and jerked my head toward the far corner. We wiggled through a sea of black leather and long hair until we were standing about four feet from a pile of amps. Mark seemed tense and completely out of place with his Gucci leather loafers and rolled-up pant legs. At least I'd gone old hippie casual with jeans, sneakers, and a vintage Doobie Brothers *Takin' It to the Streets* T-shirt. We certainly were getting some bizarre looks.

Nursing our beers, we waited out the opening band who were good for nothing more than a cover band. Mark's dark eyes flitted everywhere. I wondered if the rich boy had ever been in a biker dive bar before. Then I corrected myself. He'd not always eaten off that silver spoon he'd been born with. He'd seen hard times.

There was a short break as the stage was emptied of the first band's drums to be replaced by Chaotic Furballs' drum kit. Young women began to surge forward, filling the first several rows of fans lined up by the spacious stage. The lights suddenly went out. It was too dark to see my hand in front of my face.

Then four blue spotlights hit the stage, each glowing beam of sapphire on one member of the Furballs. The drummer, the bass player, and the lead guitarist all seemed to be cut from the same metal cloth. Wild, long hair, leather pants, no shirts, and ink tattooed into every available inch of skin. The lead singer, though, oh man, he was different. Tall and lean, he had shoulder-length black hair and a small ring in his nostril. A black tank top with black jeans that had been artfully shredded and black high tops. Silver bangles on his left wrist glistened and glittered in the blue spotlight. The crowd was deathly silent. Then the band sprang to life, hitting four chords that made the walls and floor vibrate. Colorado Penn grabbed the mic, and the women who had lined up began screaming his name as he launched into an original song about sex for sale with a strong Pantera feel to it.

Mark jerked a thumb at Colorado, and I nodded. He raised an eyebrow, but he stuck it out, sipping his beer on occasion and making a ridiculously cute face every time he took a drink.

After an hour, the band took a break, and Colorado waded through the adoring fans, male and female, to where we stood in the corner. The jukebox beside us kicked on, and an AC/DC song rocked to life.

"Outside," Colorado shouted, and we slipped into the back room with him, then out into the now dark Nevada night. "Right, so I have twenty minutes. Talk hockey to me."

He pulled up his shirt to wipe the sweat from his face. I was happy to see he'd been keeping in shape. Nothing worse than a skilled player going to seed.

"I want you to come to Arizona and try out for the Raptors."

Colorado eyed me with some suspicion. "You do recall I was suspended from playing for a year?"

"And your suspension was up as of July fourth of this year."

"Um, if no one minds, may I inquire into *why* you were suspended from playing hockey?" Mark asked, shoving his face into the conversation. Sure, it was a pretty face, but it was an owner's face, and so it should've been somewhere else while I tried to woo this man back to the ice.

"There may have been a video that included a hundred-dollar bill and two lines of cocaine," Colorado replied, and there was defiance in his bright green eyes. The kid was a firebrand. Wild yes, and chaotic at times, but one of the most sought-after rookie tenders to have ever been drafted. Pity his youth and poor choice in friends had gotten him kicked out of the game with barely a year under his belt. With the right hand, he could be a Vezina winner, I had no doubt. He just needed the right kind of coach. And that right coach was me. "It wasn't mine. I don't do drugs."

"But you were suspended," Mark said, and his jaw bottomed out somewhere around his navel.

"That was a bad call. I'd been ejected from a couple of

games before that, and they wanted to teach me a lesson."
He shrugged, and I waited for Mark to react and ask why
Colorado had been ejected. I didn't have to wait long.

"And exactly why were you ejected from games?"

"I may have spit water at a referee."

"You *may* have?"

"The Z totally deserved it."

Mark shook his head. "What the hell is a 'Z' and how
the hell did he deserve…?" He waved his hands, seemingly
lost for words.

"A Z is a ref. Y'know, the zebra stripes," I explained
when I saw Colorado frown at the question. Last thing I
needed was for him to wonder what the hell Mark was
doing here if he didn't know hockey terms.

Colorado sighed. "And if a Z calls no goaltender
interference when a guy knocks you into your net expect to
get spit at."

"You wouldn't have been ejected if you'd been on my
team. A coach stands up for his players. He doesn't throw
them under the bus."

Mark snapped his jaw shut, but oh, the thoughts were
churning inside his head. I could tell by the bubbling
brown of his eyes.

"Yeah?" Colorado asked.

"Yeah, but that's the past. And this is now. The Raptors
need you."

"No, they don't," Mark said.

Colorado looked from me to Mark, then back to me.
"Who's this Calvin Klein worshipper?"

"First of all, my clothes are not Calvin Klein. They're
Yamamoto," Mark fired back. "And second—"

"Second, we're not here to talk fashion," I interjected.

"Obviously," Mark flung back after raking Colorado
and me over with a haughty glare.

"We're here to talk hockey. Ignore him." I jerked my chin at Mark, who huffed. "We'll pay for you to fly out to Tucson and tryout."

"Oh no, we won't!" Mark was quick to say.

"Then *I'll* pay for the airline tickets. You can stay with me during training camp." Colorado thought on my offer for a moment or two. "Look, I know you're doing well here with the band, and the music is good." He cocked a sleek black eyebrow. "Okay, better than good. You could probably make it as a singer, but your first love is hockey. I read your history. I know you were in the net back home in Michigan before you were five. If you don't give it one more try with a team that's eager to sign fresh new faces, then you'll always live with the unanswered question of whether you really were as good as they all said you were."

"I'll think about it."

I nodded and handed Colorado one of my new business cards. "Fair enough. If you choose to fly out, let me know, and I'll get you set up and on the ice. You still have your gear from your stint in Jersey?"

"Yeah, I still have it." Colorado offered me his hand. We shook, and then he eased away, giving Mark a wary smile before going back inside to finish out the night.

"That went well. Want to go find our hotel room?" I walked off, hands in my front pockets, knowing he had no choice but to follow. "There are no taxis or drivers to hire out here," I added, just to let him know. "If you change your mind about standing out here all night, our room is right across the road."

I walked on, leaving him in the parking lot, grabbed my bag from the car, and strolled across the street to the Desert Dew Motel and registered. When I exited with the room key—key, not card—Mark was still in the parking lot. I waved. He gave me the finger. Chuckling to myself, I walked to our room, unlocked it, and sighed at the double bed sitting there when I'd reserved a room with two beds.

"Well, fuck," I said, then stepped into the stuffy room.

The AC came on with all due speed, and I took off my sneakers and placed them on the floor by my bag. The door flew open, and Mark blew into the cheap motel room like a hurricane. He slammed the door shut and rounded on me taking off my socks.

"You are honestly the most egotistical, stubborn, self-centered boar of a man that I have ever had the bad luck to meet! How *dare* you offer a player a tryout on the team without clearing it with anyone who actually has the right to hire and fire players?"

I pulled off sock number two, tossed them both to my sneakers, and then stood to face him. He was shaking with indignation. His curls were windblown, his cheeks thick with new whiskers, and his eyes glittering.

"You wouldn't have made the offer," I casually stated, then pulled my shirt up and over my head.

His eyes flared, then dropped to my chest before streaking back to my face. He licked his lips, and a jolt of pure grade-A lust speared me.

"Obviously not! He's like a wild badger or something. Cocaine?"

"He wasn't using."

"And spitting at people? Is that even allowed on the ice?"

"Well, goalies are different," I said, meaning no disrespect. It was just a simple truth that all tendies would agree with. I took a step closer to the disgruntled man. His tongue darted out to lick his lips again. "They tend to be given some leeway at times because of their eccentricities." He shook his head as I took another step. I paused and waited for him to speak or blink or do something other than stand there, panting, eyes wide, hands rolling and unrolling. I eased closer. His sight roamed downward, and when his eyes met mine, there was fire there, but not the kind that had been there previously. "Why don't you let me show you some of his game films before we go home tomorrow and—"

He lunged at me, his hands slapping to either side of my head and his lips grinding over mine. It startled me for a millisecond, the gnash of teeth and the hot press of soft lips, but then I felt the rush of desire race through me. I grabbed his lean waist and shoved him back just a few inches. His back hit the door, and he grunted into my open mouth. I swept in, lapping at his teeth, slipping my tongue in deeply. His reaction to my possession was to tangle his tongue with mine and tug on my hair. I leaned into him, sucking hard on his tongue, and thrust my stiff cock into his belly. A small, sweet sound of capitulation drifted out of his throat, making my balls tighten. One taste of the man had me close to coming in my shorts.

Then just as suddenly as he'd kissed me, he began pushing at me. I hated to leave the hot, wet joy of his mouth, but he slapped at my chest hard enough to force the air from me. I staggered back, chest heaving, his taste on my tongue, and watched in confusion as he ripped the door open and raced out into the night.

"Well, holy shit," I whispered as a cool wind blew into the cheap room.

SEVEN

Mark

———

I'D NEVER MOVED SO FAST, NOT even stopping to shut the motel door. I was halfway down the street before I started to breathe again and into an alley before I stopped moving.

"What the hell did I just do?" I asked the wall that was holding me up. "What in hell did I do that for?"

"You talking to yourself or me?" A growl of a voice startled me, and I jumped about a mile. Colorado stepped out of the shadows, his hands in his pockets, his long hair tangled from the wind that shoved and pushed down the narrow passageway.

"Shit," I exclaimed and leaned back to the wall with my hand fisted on my chest. "Don't sneak up on people."

Colorado crossed his arms over his chest. "You're full of rules, aren't you? Don't spit on Zs, don't do cocaine, and now don't walk down a perfectly normal alley to my own damn apartment."

"Cocaine is bad," I snapped.

"No shit, Sherlock," he countered.

My head was a mess of panic. All I could think about was whatever had taken hold of me that meant I ended up kissing Rowen, but now I had a drug-taking, spitting, former hockey goalie moving closer and blocking my exit to the dark road beyond.

"I need to go," I said in my best fake-normal voice and moved away from the wall to walk around him.

He stopped me with a hand to my chest. "Who are you?"

"Mark. I'm—"

"Rowen's latest squeeze?"

"No, god, no!"

A car door slammed somewhere on the road, and I winced. What the hell was I doing running out on a kiss, ending up in an alley, and telling weird goalies my name?

It began to rain. I felt the first drop on my cheek, and then the heavens opened.

"Come on," Colorado said and pushed at a door I hadn't even seen was there, which led back into the bar that we'd not long left. I padded in after him, and the door shut behind me, and for a moment I wondered how wise it was to follow a near stranger into a dark place. Only when he opened the door, there were other people still there, although the crowd had thinned dramatically. All I could see were the perpetual drinkers and the guy behind the bar sorting glasses.

"Two," he indicated to the barman, who didn't lecture that it was after closing hours or that he was clearing up to go home. I didn't question what Colorado had ordered two of, and found the nearest seat to plant myself on. The amber whiskey burned as I sipped it, the heat of the drink warming me from the inside.

While I drank, Colorado watched me with a focused stare that was unnerving. "Mark what?" he asked.

"Westman-Reid." I waited for him to react to the name, offering condolences for my dad, or to mention the connection to the Raptors. Instead, he showed no recognition at all and sat back in his chair to nurse his drink. He wouldn't quit with the staring. "What?" I asked when he clearly wasn't going to look away.

"Nothing," he murmured and finished his whiskey in one swallow. "You staying in town tonight?"

"Yeah."

"Motel?"

"Uh-huh." Actually I was probably going to find somewhere else. Another room at the motel maybe or a doorway, who knew?

"So, tell me, what did the wall do to you?"

"Huh?"

"When I came into the alley, you were talking to the wall."

"Not the wall, myself."

He half closed his eyes and rested his hands on his flat belly. Where the T-shirt pulled tight, I could see the muscles there, but all I could think was how could someone who hasn't played professional hockey for so long, still be in peak physical form, ready to tryout for the Raptors. Not that anything to do with the Raptors, or hockey, was front and center in my thoughts. Nope. At the moment all I could think about was the humiliating kiss I'd just planted on someone who hadn't been expecting it.

"What was it you did?" he asked.

"Did when?" I really should've paid attention to Colorado as he was talking to me. I wasn't the kind of man who zoned out. I was polite, and I listened.

"You were asking the wall for guidance on what you'd just done. What was it that you'd just done?"

Simple. I lost control of my faculties and threw myself at the sexy coach who I didn't even want to employ and who got on my last nerves with his arrogance and then looked all hot, and I just freaking lost it. That was not on my list of conversation starters. I decided that talking about hockey was a safe bet.

"So hockey *and* music? That's some combination."

He chuckled. "You're changing the subject. More whiskey?"

"No, thank you." I clasped my half-full tumbler to my chest and contemplated what the hell I was going to do next. I'd run out of that room as if my ass was on fire, and now I had to go back and either face what I'd just done head on or actually get another room at the motel and then forget this ever happened. I wanted to run, but that was just me being a coward. "Why would the Raptors be interested in you?"

He glanced up from his empty glass and shook his head. "Apparently I'm an unpolished diamond who has skills that need to be channeled. Or at least that is what some of the journalists said when they posted about how they regretted I'd fallen so badly." He laughed, but it was humorless. "Those were the charitable ones who said I had potential. The rest of the hockey press consigned me to the trash. I was hung out to dry by my coach, right at the same time an old video appeared with the cocaine. Add in the sex tape, and it was a trifecta of shit."

I swallowed. "Sex tape?"

He leaned forward and placed the glass on the table. "It wasn't exactly a sex tape, more a sex photo, only it was enough for the homophobic prick in management who decided that it was three strikes and I was out." He paused for a moment. "So, Mr. I-own-the-Raptors, is there anything else you want to ask me?"

Well, shit, and there was me thinking I had anonymity in this bar in the middle of nowhere. "You know who I am?"

"Jesus, hockey is in my blood, and you're a Westman-

Reid. Of course I know who you are, or at least I knew who your dad was. My condolences, by the way, not that your dear departed father did much for hockey. No offense."

"None taken."

"What I don't know is why you're here with Rowen for the Raptors, why you don't know what a Z was, and why in hell you were talking to a wall."

I ignored all of that and went straight for the jugular, in the most reasonable way I could think of.

"If you know I own the team, then you understand that I have the final say on hiring and firing, and I'm going to say that right now the Raptors don't want you." I tilted my chin, waiting for him to argue his point, but he sat in silence for a moment more.

"Do you want to win games, Mr. Westman-Reid?"

"Of course. The team—"

"You have too much money tied up in former big names and assholes who are destroying the Raptors. Not to mention D-men who are dead weight and leak goals like a sieve, who I wouldn't want anywhere near me. Meanwhile, I'm the best you'll get for the money you have left right now. I have potential, with a side order of fucked-up drama, plus a huge helping of lack of control. Rowen sees that. I accept that is who I am, and if the Raptors take me, I can guarantee you that you'll win some games."

Some games? I met his steady gaze. "Seems to me any goalie can say that. Hell, any player can come to me and say that with them on the team the Raptors will win games. Luck can always win games for even the shittiest team."

"Touché," the rough-and-ready rocker said, raising his left eyebrow. His gaze raked me from head to toe. "You want to get out of here?"

"To go where?" I asked and then realized immediately he wasn't suggesting we find a coffee shop or go for a walk. The carnal expression on his face was much more focused than that.

"I don't think… it wouldn't be… no, I—"

The door to the bar flew open, cold wind and rain gusting in with a disgruntled-looking Rowen, whose gaze settled on me. He stalked straight over.

"What the hell, Mark?" he asked.

I gestured with my glass. "I'm having a drink with our tryout goalie or whatever you want to call him, but he's aware now that we don't want him." I stood up so I was toe to toe with my nemesis, and he frowned at me, his gaze resting on my lips and stopping there a fraction too long. So much for him forgetting the kiss had happened.

"Yes, we do want him."

"No, we don't."

We were at an impasse, temper simmering below the surface.

Colorado stood, and pushing his long hair back from his face, he glanced from me to Rowen and back again.

"Oh, it's like that," he said with a lewd wink. "Later." He ambled toward the back door, and then it was just me, Rowen, the long-timers, and the barman.

"You seriously want him? He just drank whiskey straight down, he's got all these tattoos, and worst, he just propositioned me—"

"He's exactly what the Raptors need," Rowen interrupted.

"He had a sex tape!"

"A photo."

As far as I was concerned, that was still as bad. "And the cocaine—"

"Is bogus—"

"Everyone and their wife says the Raptors need experience—"

"And he has it, at least some of it, and we'll bring out the rest in him."

"Look, Rowen—"

"He could get us into the top twenty teams, maybe top fifteen," Rowen shouted over me. "And who knows, in two or three years, we could be contenders for the cup."

I shoved at his chest. "Keep your voice down. I'm done talking about this. My decision is final."

"We're not done yet." He gripped my hand, then pulled me to the door, straight out into the cold evening. "He's trying out. I'm not arguing, and meanwhile, what the hell was that kiss about?"

"I apologize." I used my most formal tone, and finally he let go of my hand and nodded—so that was a done deal, then. We would forget about hiring Colorado and the fact that I kissed him, and there was no need for me to worry that I'd crossed a line. He'd see my points about Colorado and do what I said. We walked back to the motel in silence, both hunched in our coats to block out the lessening rain. He unlocked the door and allowed me in first. This was all very civilized. *I can handle this.*

He shut the door, then took off his coat, and with exaggerated care, he walked toward me. He didn't touch me, but for every step back I took, he advanced one until I had my back to the door and he was just a breath away, his hand flat on the wood. His inscrutable gaze gave nothing away. Was he pissed? Aroused? *I can't tell.*

"Hands by your sides," he said softly.

"What—?"

"No touching," he growled and used his free hand to unbutton my pants, sliding the zipper down, and touching my cock with the back of his hand as my pants loosened. I was already hard. Hell, I'd been hard since he'd walked into the bar with the rain behind him, all passion and utter focus. He eased my pants down a little and then skimmed a finger under the band of my jersey shorts. Never once did he break eye contact as he slipped his hand inside and curled his fingers around my cock. My legs wobbled, but I locked myself in place. "Okay?" he asked me, and I guessed that was my chance to ask him to stop. I didn't want him to stop.

"Yeah."

He moved a little closer, not touching me anywhere except for my cock, and then he twisted his hand from root to tip, and I was embarrassingly close just with that.

"You kissed me," he said, and I felt his breath against my lips. "You're dangerous," he added and slid his hand over the length of me. "We are going to argue and butt heads, and you will hate everything I do, but after it all, I can have you up against a door, getting you off, and you won't say no."

"I should." My voice sounded husky, a little broken, and I wetted my lips in the vain hope he would kiss me. Instead he rested his forehead against mine.

"Just once," he said and quickened the pace. I fisted my hands at my sides and closed my eyes as pressure built inside me, exquisite burning pressure.

"Harder," I near whimpered and wished I could've taken the words back because I sounded desperate. His lips were so close to mine now all I needed to do was lean a quarter-inch forward, and we'd have been kissing.

"I'll get you there," he whispered, and his voice, his hand, the scent of him, it all sent me over the edge, and only when I'd finished coming did he kiss me as hard and focused as I had kissed him. I rested my hands on his hips and then went in search of his cock to get him off as well, but he chuckled into the kiss. "You really think I didn't get myself off the minute you left?"

Abruptly I was shy. Me.

Sliding my hands up and around his neck, I laced my fingers and held him there to kiss. Every muscle in my body was loose.

"First lesson in hockey. You want to know what hockey players call it when we hook up on the road?"

"What's it called?"

"Never-to-be-talked-about-again stress relief." He unhooked my hands and strode toward the bathroom. "I'm getting a shower." He shut the door firmly behind him, and I heard the lock. I guessed there was no chance of more, then. Wet, slippery, hot, sexy.

"Don't worry. I won't ever talk about this again," I said to the room. Thank god no one was here to see me do it.

I undressed and then wiped myself down with my shorts before pulling on soft cotton sleep pants. I chose the left side of the bed and climbed in, pulling the blanket up over my chin and turning on my side to face the wall. I heard the shower stop, closed my eyes, and listened to him come out of the bathroom and get into bed. I didn't think for one minute he'd pull me in for a snuggle—after all, this was just stress relief, as he'd termed it.

Anyway, I was tired, and it wasn't as if I was attracted to him in any way.

Liar.

EIGHT

Rowen

IT WAS one of those days…

I'd stubbed my toe after getting out of bed, tripped over a janky bit of elevated sidewalk during my run and skinned my knee, burned my toast, got soap in my eye in the shower, and got a fucking Pepsi instead of a Dr Pepper at the soda machine in the players' lounge. Oh, and Colorado's flight had been delayed, so he'd probably miss the first preseason game against Dallas. The only good thing so far had been the arrival of my new associate coach, who I was going to introduce to the team as soon as I could get my stupid laptop to stop doing updates.

"Okay, screw my little wordy welcome thing for the press release." I slapped the lid down and gave the updates a middle finger. Then I stalked out of my office to find Terri and make the intro. She was ensconced in her office, unpacking personal items when I knocked on the open door. "You ready for this?"

"Of course." She nibbled at her lower lip as we walked to the Raptors' dressing room.

"For what it's worth, you look great in the Raptors

colors," I said, then gave her a smile. It was the truth. The hockey world was going to love her once they got over themselves.

She tugged down her shiny new red Raptors jacket, nodded, and ceased gnawing on her lower lip. Rounding the corner, we then skidded to a halt when two players rolled out into the corridor, fists flying. I shoved Terri behind me, then bolted down the hall to grab hold of Alejandro and jerk him away from Aarni Lankinen. Both men were half dressed, hockey pants and pads, sans jersey and skates, and Ryker Madsen was right in the middle of things, trying to get them to calm down.

Alex was incensed. Nostrils flared, breathing rapid, bulging brown eyes, he took another swing at Lankinen getting to his feet and managed to clip him in the side of the head. Aarni lunged at Alex, and it took all I had to keep them separated until four other players got involved.

"What the *hell* is going on here?" I barked. Arms around Alex to keep him from lashing out. I walked the irate rookie backward several paces and placed him against the cement wall.

A stream of rapid-fire Spanish flew over my shoulder at Aarni. I gave the kid another shove, just enough to jar him out of his mindset, I hoped.

"Fucker, miserable fucking asshole," Alex snarled through gritted teeth. I pinned him to the wall again, one hand on his shoulder, the other pointing at the fracas with Aarni taking place behind me.

"Someone better speak up and do it now!" I shouted, and that raised voice seemed to sink into at least one brain.

"We were listening to one of Alex's playlists while gearing up," Madsen stated, his voice big and strong in the packed hallway. "Nothing bad or rude, just some Aventura, Luis Fonsi, Daddy Yankee…"

"That fucker," Alex growled, pointing back to Aarni, I assumed. "He said that if I wanted to listen to beaner music, I should haul my ass back to Mexico and do it quick before the wall is finished and I never get back in!"

My jaw would have hit my chest had it not been clenched so tightly. See, this shit right there was why Aarni needed to go. He was a toxic lake poisoning everyone who came in contact with his polluted shores. But oh no, the high and mighty Mark Westman-Reid and his billionaire siblings were too busy doing who knows what to even grace us here in the trenches with a visit over the past week. Sure, they peeked in from high above, hiding in the owners' box as the grunts did the hard work of trying to polish up this turd of a team. Probably sitting up there sipping high-priced bubbly and talking tariffs and tax breaks with leaders of the Young Republicans. Hell, maybe they were trying to lure a new GM in to replace the one who resigned just two days ago due to "internal differences with the new owners."

"I never said that," Aarni shouted behind me. I shook that finger again, never looking back at the talking canker sore. "I never did. He's a fucking liar."

Alex wriggled to get free. I pressed on his shoulder harder and glowered at him. That seemed to calm his rightfully angry jets for a moment.

"Both of you are sitting out the game tonight," I informed them.

"What? Why am *I* being benched? He was the one who used a slur!" Alex railed.

"He did, and you jumped him instead of coming to me or one of the other coaches to report the offensive language. Fighting things out may have worked under your old coach, but it does not fly with me," I told the bodies packed in the corridor. I dared Alex to say a word with my incredibly mad eyebrows. He wanted to, I could see it, but he bit back what was on his tongue, then nodded. Aarni, the moron, had to keep running his mouth. I glanced back at him over my shoulder and gave him the same look I'd silenced Alex with. He fell silent, but I could see the bubbling resentment just under the surface. The sooner that bag of skating shit was gone from this team, the better. Time for me and Mark to have another talk, and this time, there would be no fucking hand jobs or wet kisses. "I will not tolerate racism, homophobia, or sexism in this building."

I stepped back from Alex, who, even though he was still panting and tense, was in control.

"This is the first and only time I will say this. Anytime I hear of anything offensive being said about a fellow player's heritage, religion, or sexual orientation, I will slap the offender down so hard their great-grandchildren will feel it."

The players mumbled and nodded, skulking back into the dressing room. Madsen tossed an arm around Alex's shoulder and led him away. When the hall was emptied of players, I spent a solid minute raking my fingers through my hair, then turned to find Terri standing in the corner by a coffee machine, blue eyes wide. Well, fuck. That was a great first impression.

"Is it too late to change my mind?" she asked, pushing out from the wall with what appeared to be some sass in her walk.

"You signed the papers, so yes—it is too late."

"Well, damn. Guess I better go say hi to the team, then." She squared her shoulders and tossed her ponytail over her shoulder. "Woman coming in! Drop your socks and cover your cocks!"

And into the dressing room she sauntered, large as life.

I chuckled at the shouts and gasps and squeaks from the men, then lingered in the doorway, arms folded, as she made herself known to the guys. My gaze rested on Aarni, for he was simmering and ugly-looking. Wisely, if he had a comment to make, he kept it to himself. Most of the men stumbled over shy greetings, eyes wide in obvious shock.

"I think they like me," Terri said after the short meet and greet. "Shall we go find the rest of the coaching staff and watch them fumble for words too?"

I fell into my best Bogie impersonation. "Louis, I think this is the beginning of a beautiful friendship."

She chuckled, then began humming "As Time Goes By," which kind of cemented the whole friendship thing right there and then.

Truthfully, given how this Tuesday had started, I should have assumed the general shittiness would carry on right through our first game of the year. No one expected much from preseason games. They were basically televised scrimmages as we coaches worked at whittling down our rosters from about forty hopefuls to our final twenty-three, which we had to submit to the league as "Opening Day Playing Rosters". Which was all fine and good because we had about three weeks to thin things down. I already had a mental checklist of problematic players and had made a note to myself to track down Mark and have a talk with him ASAP.

It seemed odd to me that two men could work in the same building and not see each other at all. Not that I wanted to see Mark. Sure, we'd had a bit of fun on that trip to meet Terri and Colorado. We'd made out, and he'd fallen against that door with a soft sigh that I still heard and replayed whenever I was in the shower with a stiff dick in my hand. Sadly, that stiff dick was mine. Mark's dick had been lots more fun to stroke, but that was just that—fun. Nothing more and nothing less. Two horny men in a dingy motel. Passions and anger flared. He kissed me. I jerked him off. We went to bed. Simple and clean with no histrionics. Mark had been quiet on the flight home, which suited me because I had a team to build and had little time for relationships. I blinked when the R-word flittered into my thoughts. The voice of the woman singing the national anthem became white noise for a second or two. One hot hand job did not a relationship make. Or even a friendship. In truth, I disliked the man. He was too pretty, too rich, too well dressed, too rich, too prone to being a snob, too rich, and too kissable. Which seemed to be the case for those model types; lips to die for but a personality to avoid. Whatever. Who cared about him? Not me. I had a team to build and no time for fashion models who tasted like honey fresh from the comb. Not that I liked honey much either. Or combs. Hated combs. I closed my eyes, inhaled deeply, and exorcised his highness from my mind.

I stood behind my players, my nerves a bit frayed despite how I tried to appear nonplussed—this *was* my first game as a professional coach—with a woman at my side as my second-in-command. Her short press conference with Jason Westman-Reid after lunch had sent shockwaves through the sporting world. The Raptors' front office had been inundated with emails and texts from men in utter outrage over this woman daring to intrude on this last bastion of maleness and testosterone. I hoped Terri had not read the comments on any of the social media posts from the team, which were kind of shitty, to be honest. Guess the rebuild should include some new blood for the

Twitter, Instagram, and Facebook followers, but that wasn't my fish to fry.

Dallas was just as creaky and sloppy as we were in the first period. We'd all done some research on the team after Terri had been welcomed into the Raptors coaching family by Art, Craig, and Todd. She'd been quick on the uptake, grasping what I wanted from the players, and eager to start passing along the fine points of my coaching style and team dynamic of speed of hand, speed of foot, and speed of mind. My two healthy scratches, Alex and Aarni, were up in the owners box, which was fine. Terri was already hustling around, passing along my thoughts and scribbling down new plays on her whiteboard. The fans had been lukewarm and thin, only half the seats filled, but again, that was normal for preseason games.

The second period tightened up a bit when we first came back out. There were small flashes of personality and talent here and there. The rookies were all nerved up, and I could see how they were struggling to make the adjustment from collegiate hockey to professional hockey. Rink size variances in the NCAA and collegiate ranks was one example; others were rules differences such as hand passes in the defensive zone, pucks shot directly out of play in the defensive zone, goal scored during a delayed penalty, and overtime and tie game variances.

I'd studied hard myself since putting my name to that contract, and I expected the kids to know the differences as well.

"Good effort," I told the second line as it rolled back over the bench. "I want to see more effort on the defensive side of your game, Sam." He nodded as sweat ran off the end of his nose. "When I see you back-checking with your legs straight, that tells me you're not putting in enough effort. Your whole line plays defense, right? It's not just the two D-men out there. When the puck is in our zone, you cannot let defense become an afterthought. Don't slow down on the forecheck."

Ryker, who played on the second line with Sam Bennett and Lucas Polisnki for now, bobbed his head in agreement, then leaned into Sam and began talking at him about this thing that Tennant Rowe had told him about how all coaches see the lazy game and they hate it. Which was true. I could spot a lazy player a mile away, and lazy players did not make my teams.

"Coach, there's a call from security for you," Terri said, passing along her cell phone to me. I refused to have my phone with me during a game. Anyone who knew me knew that I hated cell phones in the barn almost as much as I hated lazy players.

I took the phone from her hand, turned from the bench, and placed the Samsung to my ear.

"Coach C, this is Drew, head of security, and we have a person of questionable persuasion here at the player's entrance telling us that he's supposed to be playing goalie for you tonight? And sure, he has funky red goalie pads and helmet, but, Coach, this kid looks to be about as far from a hockey player as I am the Duchess of Sussex."

A mental image of the massive black man with the winning smile who sometimes worked the players' entrance rose up and made me happy. Drew was a good guy and better than some of the security this team had in place. Also, I was smiling because my new goalie had somehow managed to get here in time to play the second half. Thank God. I'd penciled his name in just in case.

"Is he surly looking with shaggy black hair and tattoos and says he's named after a state?" I shouted over the roar of someone scoring a goal. When I glanced back to see, it was Dallas celebrating down by our net.

"Oh yeah," Drew replied.

"Let him in and show him to the dressing room. I need him up here in six minutes." I ended the call and gave Terri her phone back. "That phone is not to come to the bench with you again," I informed her and got a stunned look for a second before she gave me a curt nod.

Andre Lemans, our man in net, was shaken a bit but not overly upset. He was a steady sort of guy, nothing flashy, but a solid backup sort of goalie. If we could corral Colorado and get him to take the bit, he'd be one of the pieces of this new team rebuild.

The first line had a good shift, getting a nice flurry of shots on goal that never snuck through the massive man in net for Dallas. The second line rolled over the boards in unison, and I watched closely as the three forwards and two defensemen fell into a nice, tight forechecking pattern, Sam keeping on his man as Dallas made a foray into our zone. I suspected matching Ryker with Alex would be a prime pairing, but we'd not see that tonight as Alex was riding the bench. The puck was lobbed into the corner, and a small skirmish erupted as a knot of players battled to free the puck. Sam got his shoulder into the back of the Dallas captain, pinning him to the glass, and shoved the puck to Ryker, who spun and shuttled it out to Vladislav Nokikov, a burly bear of a Russian, who played defense with a drive that had made him legendary. He was an older player, grizzled and vocal, who played a clean but physical game. His greatest joy in life, it seemed, was throwing big hits and shoulder checks to anyone who dared to skate up on him.

Vlad set off down the ice, a locomotive of a man, eyes on the Dallas net, and took a slapshot that rang off the pipes and got a small "Ahhh" from the meager crowd. The forwards hit the Dallas end, Madsen falling on the puck as soon as it hit the ice in front of the Dallas crease. He kept his shoulder down and dug that puck free from a bigger and more experienced Dallas winger, kicking it off his skate to his stick, then ramming it past the goalie with sheer determination. The goal horn sounded, and Madsen threw his arms into the air as his linemates surrounded him to beat on his helmet.

"Nicely done!" I shouted to the line as they returned to the bench. Then Colorado arrived from the tunnel, and a kind of stunned hush fell over the rink as fans and the Tucson area local sports network got their first look at Colorado Penn on the Raptors' bench. He sat there for two minutes, and then a TV time-out was called, and we made the goalie change.

"Uhm, Rowen?" That was Art Schaffer, my goalie coach. "Is this a surprise birthday present for me because if it is, I'll be honest and say I wish you'd have shopped at a different store."

I glanced over at Art. "Is today your birthday?"

"No, it's in May."

I grinned and clapped him on the back. "Well then, happy early birthday. Let's see what he can do, shall we?"

Art looked reluctant, to say the least. I settled back onto my heels, glanced up over my shoulder at the owners' box, and gave the uppity-mucks lounging around in there a smart little salute as Colorado Penn settled into the crease. Cue royal meltdown in the posh seats. This should be good.

NINE

Mark

"WHAT THE FUCK?" I stood from my seat so fast that I stumbled forward and ended up gripping the barrier at the front of our box. I couldn't believe what I was seeing. When I saw the name flash on the Jumbotron, it didn't even click what was happening, and then TV time-out was done and abruptly the Raptors were putting in a new goalie.

Not just a new goalie.

Colorado *freaking* Penn.

"What's wrong?" Leigh asked. She was crammed into a corner with a blocked view—it seemed the previous owners weren't that hot on accessibility. I'd already made a mental note for changing that to be a priority, but right now, that was pushed way down under my shock at seeing the long-haired rocker going out onto *our* ice. Not to mention that Rowen looked up and gestured to us. Or me. Whatever. That cocky bastard actually put his hand to his head and saluted the box.

"Can he do that?" I snapped and turned to face Jason and Cam. "Did you authorize this shit?"

Cam glanced at me with a bored expression on his face. "Sorry?"

"Did we do what now?" Jason asked.

I pointed wordlessly down at the ice, unable to form a sentence that included our coach's name or that of our new goalie.

Jason frowned and glanced down. "What?" he asked again.

"I explicitly told him—I told him—and you—did you—?"

"Use your words, Marky-Mark," Cam said and stared back down at his phone.

"Don't freaking call me that," I snapped. He damn well knew I hated it when he used the nickname he'd had for me when we were kids.

"Whatever," he said and yawned theatrically. Fucker.

"Talk to me," Jason said and touched my shoulder. I shrugged him off and saw the flash of hurt in his eyes. Well, I wasn't here to make things good for my asshole brothers, so he could forget it if he thought I'd let them touch me.

"You know what," I said with emotion, "if you three are going to leave this all to me, then I'm out of here."

Jason was about to grab my arm, but I slid from out of his grasp and left the box.

"Mark, wait!" I evaded Jason and headed down the steps to the main corridor, passing out of security, and followed signs to the main concourse. My card got me everywhere, and by the time the game had finished, an uninspiring four-one loss, with the new goalie letting three by, I was in Rowen's office, leaning on his desk and waiting for him. I resolved to sit calmly and process everything so that I was in a better frame of mind when he arrived. It didn't matter how long he took to get his ass down there after his pep talk or whatever crap he fed the players to make them feel better than they were.

I pulled up the finances on my phone again. I'd spent all day looking at them, trying to get a feel for where the leaks were, and I didn't have to be a financial genius to see that we were hemorrhaging money. No business survived when expenses outweighed income. Two of the biggest sponsors, Maddock Foods and Phoenix Datacom, had pulled advertising and sponsorship, and there was nothing in the pipeline to replace them.

I'd forwarded the details to Cam, Jason, and Leigh. I'd received a detailed response filled with positive wording from Cam, and a GIF of an ostrich with its head in the sand from Jason. Leigh at least sent me the truth, with a strongly worded we-know-we're-in-trouble email. About the only thing I could draw from my family's responses was that Cam was hopeful, Leigh was a realist, and Jason was a fuck-headed asshole.

Anger began to build inside me again. I should have stayed in New York. The team meant nothing to me. In fact no one there meant anything to me. This family didn't want me, not really, except maybe Leigh.

Breathe. Calm the hell down. I breathed through my anger, recalled the moments of serenity I'd had, focused, and finally I had everything in place. My family and this team would not destroy the life I had carefully constructed for myself. More importantly, Rowen Carmichael needed to stop messing with my head, and I had to tell him that now.

"No, breathe, calm... peace..." I murmured and counted back from a hundred.

I'd gotten to thirty-seven when he walked in, and the minute I saw him, all my calm fled, and my anger spilled out as a way to defend my hurting heart.

"I explicitly told you that Colorado was not to be given any sort of tryout."

He sidestepped me and went around his desk, shrugging off his suit jacket and hanging it on the back of his chair. "Uh-huh," he said, in that infuriating nonchalant tone, which was guaranteed to get my back up.

"But you did it anyway."

He glanced at me. "Are you done?"

What? Done? I was nowhere near done, and the last vestige of control flew out the window.

"It's not bad enough that he was filmed with drugs, but he was drinking whiskey at the bar as though it was water, he's unfit for this team, and if you're not going to listen to my valuable insights, then why the hell are you even here? Your arrogance that you think you know better is beyond belief. Did you not even see the goals he allowed?" I waved my phone. "Believe me, I didn't even have to be there to see them, because they were posted in all their glory on Twitter. Do you know what the hashtags are? Do you?"

"I bet you're going to tell me."

"Losers. Failures. Cocaine. Drugs. And my favorite? Craptors."

He nodded. "I see what they did there." He sounded amused.

"What? You think it's funny?"

He huffed and looked thoughtful. "Well, it's pretty far from genius adding a C to Raptors, but yeah—"

"For God's sake, do you not realize social media can be our enemy as easy as it can be our friend? Do you even want this team to survive? How can you give Colorado a tryout?"

"Okay, you want to do this here? Did you actually reread the contract between me and the Raptors?" he asked in a tone that was eerily gentle.

"Every single time you do something wrong, you throw that back in our faces—"

"Your father seemed very happy to—"

"My father was an asshole who didn't know his puck from his latest fuck." *Fuck, now I'm rhyming shit.* I stalked to him and poked at his chest. "This whole team was just a tax write-off for him, and the stipulation in his will was a way to manipulate me into coming back. This team is nothing special, and it won't get any better with you pulling this kind of stunt."

"Hiring Colorado is not a stunt," Rowen said and pushed my hand away. "You need to go now before I do something I'll regret." His eyes glittered dangerously, but there was no way I was walking out of this office before we had the hierarchy set in stone.

"You report to us, we hired you to do a job, and so far you've contracted a new coach who could end up being more of a liability with the amount of negative reaction we've seen on social media to her being a woman. You've offered a tryout to an alcoholic, drug-taking goalie who can't stop pucks, even if the net was four inches across and hidden in his ass. And as for you? You have no cohesive plan in place and seem to have no idea what you're doing."

My hands were in fists at my sides. I was breathing heavily. I'd lost my cool, but it wasn't just Rowen who'd turned my temper up to eleven. It was Cam and his stupid nickname, the lack of respect from him, and dark memories of my less than stellar childhood smashed into me. Then it was Jason and his hurt expression, and the fact that I was tired, and I needed to go back to New York, and the man in front of me was messing with my equilibrium. Everything was piling on me, and I'd even thought it was a good idea to kiss him. I was out of control, and he wasn't doing a damn thing to help.

"Are you finished? Because you can go now." He was deceptively calm. I could see the temper flashing in his eyes, but he was relaxed, and his hands weren't in fists like mine.

"That's it?" I couldn't believe what I was hearing. "You're not going to defend yourself?"

He tilted his head a little and frowned. "Oh, is that what you want me to do? Do you need me to defend my position? Do you want the statistics, the research, the scouting reports, drug tests, experience, personal recommendations, and most of all a detailed list of my gut feelings? Would that help you feel a bigger man?"

The fact that he was so calm was like waving a red flag in front of a bull. I wanted him to lose his control. I wanted him to push me up against the door and demand that I retract what I'd said, and then tell me I was wrong. At least anger and accusations would be reactions I could handle.

"Coach?" I whirled to face the person who'd dared to come into the office when I was there, belatedly realizing that the door was wide open and that anyone could have heard our discussion. It wasn't just one person. It was Terri, her eyes wide, and her lips in a set line, and alongside her, Colorado himself. He looked like a deer in the headlights, part defensive, but stunned.

Very deliberately, Terri pushed Colorado inside and shut the door behind them.

"First, both of you, shut the damn door if you're going to bicker, or you'll destroy what's left of team morale," she snapped. "Colorado is here to submit his latest test results." She placed a printout on Rowen's desk. "The tests he himself volunteered to do at least once a day for the time he's trying out with us so there's absolutely no blowback on the team for what he was alleged to be part of."

"And for the record, I did not hire a groupie to pee on me or in a cup for me," Colorado tossed out rather blithely. "We save that for the tour bus. Not that Binks, the drummer, would appreciate me talking about his kink but eh." He shrugged a well-padded shoulder.

"There was—"

"I haven't finished," she interrupted and turned to face me head on, six inches shorter, but I had no doubt that right this moment she would take me out. "Mr. Westman-Reid, what I have between my legs does not determine my ability to do my job. If I hear anything like that again from you or any of the management team, players, or staff, I will sue you and this sorry ass team for every cent you have."

"I was talking about your impact on social media—"

She ignored me, gripped Colorado's arm, and tugged him outside, slamming the door shut behind her. Rowen stared at me, his expression closed, and I ran out of steam. Something about the way Terri had spoken to me, demanding respect, made me hot and cold with misery and shame.

"You can go," Rowen repeated to dismiss me and picked up Colorado's results, pushing them into a folder with the Raptors logo on the front. I'd always thought it was a pretty cool logo, the eagle or whatever it was holding a hockey stick, but I didn't say that.

In fact, I couldn't say anything.

I left without saying anything else, worked my way back up to staff parking, and walked toward my car.

"Cam's sorry," Jason said from the shadows by the car.

"I'm not—" Cam began but stopped with a muffled oomph where I assumed Jason thumped him. "Sorry I called you Marky-Mark," Cam then added after a moment's pause, with an air of boredom to his voice. Marky-Mark had started out life as an affectionate nickname, for when Cam and I had been close. He called me Monkey; I called him Cools. Born close together, we'd done everything together as kids, taking turns to tease and torment Jason with him being four years older than Cam.

Monkey and Cools—that was us, inseparable until I'd begun to accept who I truly was. Then Monkey had become Marky, and worse, and abruptly I'd never had anything but loathing thrown at me from Cam.

"I don't give a shit what you call me, asshole." I continued to my car, with Jason shadowing me.

"Please don't go," he pleaded.

"I'm tired. I need sleep." *I need to process the incalculable temper that is inside me, the hate and frustration that is bubbling up in every molecule of me. But most of all, I need to think about the chaotic feelings that just seeing Rowen cause me.*

"You can't go back to New York yet," Jason said, but he wasn't telling me; he was imploring. "Give the team a chance to leave a legacy that matters."

I stopped. "I never said I was going back to New York."

Jason moved closer to me, and I could see the confusion in his expression. "You said in the box you were leaving…"

"No, I said… shit… I'm tired, and I'm going back to the hotel."

I was almost in my car when Jason stopped me with something I never thought I'd hear. "You're welcome to use the house. I'm not there, Cam isn't, and with Mom away, it would just be you and Leigh."

"I'm fine where I am," I lied. After all, despite it being a nice hotel, it wasn't the home I had in my city apartment, with the things I'd chosen to surround myself with. I'd built a life there. I had as many friends as a former model-turned-business owner. The modeling industry is fickle, and friendships are few and far between.

"If you don't want to be at the house, we have a spare room at our place," Jason carried on. "Amelia would love to have you stay there, and you could get to know the kids. Lewis was asking after you last night."

"Wow, you must be desperate to use your kids to get me to stay."

"I wasn't. Jesus, Mark, whatever happened in the past, we're your brothers."

I snorted in disbelief. "Pity you're only remembering the past now that you need me for something."

I settled into the low-slung car seat and locked the door, not even looking back in my rearview mirror as I left Cam and Jason. The Lamborghini ate the miles to my hotel, but it gave me no joy.

All I could think of was that at some point this evening, I'd let the past get inside my head. I'd been a pompous asshole, and I was the last person to devalue what a woman could do for this team. I hadn't meant for it to come across as misogynistic bullshit. I was just the one who could see the bottom line. Twitter mentions meant income; it was simple as that. A round of shitty tweets and we might lose tickets, and we were already hanging on by the fingertips while the mountain of debt was growing daily. We needed investors, and fast, if we were going to meet our contractual obligations. Otherwise at the end of this season, there wouldn't be a Raptors team at all.

All I could see were negatives, and I restarted the engine and drove away from the hotel, heading for the Catalina foothills. After an hour of driving aimlessly, lost in thought, I felt my shoulders fall a little, and the tension headache began to ease. By the time I ended up back at the hotel, I had a list of things I needed to do.

Most importantly, Terri deserved an apology and my respect for her achievements. Everyone had said a former model wouldn't have the brains to start their own agency, and I'd shown them I wasn't the person I'd been pigeon-holed as. I'd fought and scratched for respect, and she was having to do the same thing. I only had to see the social media mentions to understand the vitriol thrown at her. She needed me to understand she was a kick-ass coach and nothing more.

I guessed I should cut Colorado some slack, for at least one more game. Maybe he'd shine next time he was on the ice, although I wasn't holding my breath.

I had to sit down and have a balanced conversation with Rowen, make him see my worries, and attempt to listen rationally to his answers. Then I needed to get him into a suit and set up some sponsorship meetings before it didn't matter what the team did on the ice at all.

I buried my head on my crossed arms, breathing in the leather scent of the car, and realized I had to work my way back to my family.

It could've been that Jason wasn't just using his son Lewis as bait.

Lewis might want to know me, and maybe I could be an uncle for real.

I'm so scared.

TEN

Rowen

"... net front presence is low. I'm just not seeing the drive that I'd like, but final call is yours, Rowen."

I snapped back from a mental meander I'd taken, my usually focused mind drifting to touch on that cryptic missive from the princeling last night about a damn meeting this morning.

"Sorry, I was contemplating something else." I picked up the latest analytics and perused them. "Agreed, we can send Henry Laboutin down to Tampa if we don't see some real improvement by the third game. I'm liking what I'm seeing from Madsen and Garcia." I passed the latest readouts to Terri, who yawned, using the papers to shield her gaping mouth before passing them along to Art, who was reading some new stats on the goalies in camp. "What I'm looking for from them right now is skill, attitude, character, preparedness, and a willingness to follow my program." I glanced at my watch. I had ten minutes to wrap up this staff meeting before taking the elevator to the executive suites to meet some potential sponsor. "I'm not seeing any of those qualities in Lankinen."

Everyone in the small room grunted in agreement. Terri yawned again, then whispered an apology. "Late night." She smirked and gave us a wink.

"Yeah, for me too. Managed to make it to ten before I fell asleep in the recliner. Never let it be said married life isn't all glitter and paparazzi," Art said, getting a small round of guffaws from the five of us. "Speaking of glitter and paparazzi." My goaltending coach looked right at me.

I lifted a hand. "Let me guess, Colorado Penn?"

"The Jared Leto of the crease," Art replied dryly. Terri, Craig, and Todd all snorted in amusement with me. "The kid is a sieve of late, but I think I'm seeing where his problems are."

"Mm, don't we all? He's got a great glove hand, but his reactions are slow as molasses in January. That will sharpen with time back on his skates," I said.

"Agreed, but he's too rangy. I like to see an aggressive goalie at times, but he's a drifter. He needs to stay put a bit. I like how he handles the puck, he's damn good, and that will be an asset, but he needs to keep his ass at home. I'm going to start working with him on that. Also, he tends to paddle down a bit too quickly, but that's nothing that we can't fix. His mindset is here and on the game despite the number of groupies showing up for morning skates."

Yes, the Penn Patrol. A growing number of young women—and plenty of men—who were flocking to the rink every time the players showed up. They were a ratty-looking bunch who were now singing lyrics from John Denver or Joe Walsh songs every time Colorado was on the ice. The shouts of "COLORADO" when they got to the chorus of "Rocky Mountain High" echoed off the rafters every time Penn made a move. I found it to be amusing in its own way. Rock groupies screaming, holding up signs, and dancing to the music they carried with them—Chaotic

Furball songs I was sure—at hockey games were unique but harmless. Penn enjoyed the attention obviously, and a few local news shows had touched on it, so that was good, right?

"Okay, so we're set on Penn starting the next game?" I asked and got a nod from my goalie coach. "Good. Next on the agenda is a small item that came down from the stratosphere just this morning. It seems that the team will be announcing that Jason Westman-Reid will be the new interim general manager." I rolled my eyes, then glanced from Terri to Art to Craig and Todd.

Todd sighed theatrically. "Isn't there some sort of law about nepotism?" our lanky video coach enquired.

"If only," I replied, stretching out my legs under the round table. "We're just going to have to deal with the Three Stooges bumbling about until they can find someone with an ounce of sense to take the job."

"Well, in all honesty," Craig began, then paused to lift a sugar-coated doughnut from the dozen box that sat in the middle of the table. "He can't make worse decisions than old brass-bottom Bergner. I've had the dubious honor of trying to work with some of the washed-up shit he signed over the past ten years. Glory contracts that blew our cap space to hell as he picked up old players who were past their prime in some vain hope of getting into the playoffs. Also, if I may point out, Bergner was the brilliant baboon who not only headhunted Aarni but offered him a no-trade clause as well."

Craig took a huge bite out of his doughnut and chewed aggressively. His dislike of one of his core defensemen spoke volumes. Craig Millerson was a big, jovial man who loved his D-men as much as they loved him. He'd played the game for close to twenty years, and he knew his shit. Not that you'd be aware of any of the skill the coaching staff had given some of the malignant and misguided players we were saddled with.

"Well, Lankinen is an ongoing cyst on my balls but—what?" I asked when Terri drew back with a look of horror.

"Far too vivid an image for my sleepy brain," she stated. The men laughed along in agreement with her. "I think we all can agree that the sooner Aarni is gone, the better. Can we send him down to the minors?"

"Sure, if he acts up enough to warrant disciplinary action. Terri, I want you to walk around the rink in a string bikini until he says something sexist," I teased.

"Rumor has it he likes the guys just as much as the girls, so why don't *you* walk around in a Speedo until he spouts off?" she fired right back. I loved this girl.

"If I were straight, I'd marry you," I told her, which brought an awkward kind of silence to the room. "Okay, so I kind of just outed myself. That information stays here in this room." I glanced from one set of wide eyes to another. They all bobbed their heads. "Thank you. It's not that I feel any kind of shame over being gay. It's just that this team does not need a media firestorm of the kind that blew down on Tennant Rowe when he came out."

"Would it be okay to admit something here?" someone asked and we all nodded. "If I were gay, I'd marry you just so we could name our first child Hoagy."

"Ass," I said after I was done laughing. Someone's phone rang. I gave the room a low glower. I truly hated cell phones at times. When it continued to chirrup, I deepened my scowl.

"It's you," Terri said and pointed at my phone lying by the coffee pot in the corner of the staff lounge.

"I knew that. I was just testing out my coach glower." I

coughed, smiled sweetly to the chortles, and then pushed to my feet to answer my damn phone.

"You're late," Mark snapped into my ear.

"I'll be up in five," I told him and severed the call. That had been the first time I'd heard his voice in close to a week. He'd stayed well clear of the lower depths of the barn since his blowup after our first game. I thought he might bless us with his presence after our second loss, but nope. "I have this thing to do."

I lifted my Raptors jacket from the back of my chair. The others in the room got up as well, and we filed out into the hall, passing players ambling in for morning skate, T-shirts, running shorts, and sneakers the norm. Coming to games, they had to be suited, but not for skates or other informal meetings.

"We'll put them through their paces," Terri assured me as we made our way to the elevator that would carry me to heaven, aka the owners' box and executive suites. "Maybe grab a seat when the meet and greet is done and observe from high up?"

"That was my plan." I gave her a wink and stepped into the elevator when the door slid open. I envied them the ice time. Playing suck-up with rich people was not my cup of tea. I wished I had grabbed a Dr Pepper on the way to the elevator. The doors opened, and I stepped out onto a thick carpet of deepest red. Hard times for the team showed down below, but up here, it was luxury as usual. Private doors all locked tightly hid corporate suites that cost hundreds of thousands of dollars. Some had bars and servers and buffets. But that was fine. These suits were coughing up the big cash to sit up there and pretend to watch hockey. It was the grandeur of the owners' box that stopped me dead when I sauntered in unannounced.

The box was stunning. Soft desert colors of rust and

tan and deep red could be seen in the carpeting and designer couches. A full bar with a bartender in attendance and a kitchen with a cook who was preparing crepes, by the looks of it. One wall was thick glass that looked down on the ice; the other held a massive viewing screen. Seated at one of the thick oaken tables by the glass wall were Mark and two older white men in dark suits.

"Sorry I'm late. I was doing my job," I said as I walked past the slim black man in white chef garb whipping eggs with bits of scallion in it.

"So was I," Mark replied, and they all stood. "Rowen Carmichael, this is Robert and Clark Lake. They own Catalina Foothills Chrysler Plymouth. They're interested in becoming corporate sponsors and expressed an interest in meeting our new coach over breakfast."

"Ah," I said and switched from coach mode to ass-kissing mode, my least favorite mode, to be sure. I knew it was all part of the game. Even in college athletics, we'd had to bow and scrape to the all-mighty dollar. "I've seen your commercials."

"I hope you think of us when you're looking for a new vehicle. We own fourteen dealerships scattered all over the state, with ten in New Mexico," Robert said as we shook hands.

"As a matter of fact, I need a car. I sold mine before moving out here and have always had a soft spot for Chryslers. My grandfather owned a fifty-six sky-blue Chrysler Imperial he said he wanted to be buried in. Grandma had other plans of course."

That made the car guys laugh and clap me on the shoulder. The tension around Mark's eyes and mouth lessened, and by the time we were done with our crepes, Mark seemed almost relaxed. That was until our new sponsors left and it was me and Mark alone in the owners' box, the smell of fried onions and fresh coffee still thick in the air.

I sat there sipping incredibly rich coffee with cream as my men worked out down below me. Mark kept shifting around in his seat as he tapped away on his phone.

"Ryker Madsen comes to me every day and asks what he can do for the team," I said into my coffee as Terri and the Raptors worked on improving our forecheck. Mark glanced up from his phone, dark eyes wary and nodded.

"That's good."

"Mm, yeah, it is. Alejandro is watching daily videos of his time on ice."

"That's also good."

"It is. Would you like to know what Aarni Lankinen is doing to improve himself?"

His gaze touched mine briefly. He knew the answer. It was nothing. Aarni did nothing that was above or beyond. Yes, he was a fine player, but the toxicity he cast around outweighed the nice goal tallies he'd racked up, at least in my book.

"His situation isn't as cut-and-dry dried as you'd like it to be. He has a contract, and as you like to point out at every available opportunity, it's pretty iron-clad, just like yours. But we're hoping to open up discussions with his agent and possibly see about moving him to another team before he becomes a free agent. We'd like to get a few pennies out of him if we can."

"And when does he become a free agent?"

"Two years."

"For fuck's sake," I groaned. "Your father and your ex-GM were asses. The only wise thing your dad did was get me here."

"Conceited much?"

"Honest." I studied his face closely. His eyes were

engrossing, so dark and expressive. And that mouth of his was enticing. "Here's another bit of honesty for you. I think about our hookup in that cheap hotel room every night."

His eyes flared, and some color rushed into his face. "No, you don't."

That made me snort softly. "Listen to you, such an autocrat, telling me that I don't think of you when I jerk off at night when you know that I do because you do the same thing. You think of me when you're alone in bed with your cock in your hand. You think of me, and you wonder what it would be like. You're thinking of it right now. You're wondering what it would be like if I pressed your back to this table, put your ankles on my shoulders, and fucked you so well and so hard you'd not be able to recall your name."

He licked his upper lip and shook his head, but no words fell out of him. I leaned back to ease the strain of hard dick against cold zipper.

"We're here to talk about hockey. Colorado Penn is a—"

"Is a highly skilled goalie who hasn't played professionally for a year. Give him time to get his groove back. He's also testing clean daily, which, if you ask me, is above and beyond for the man to do, and yet you're riding me about his presence on the team. Just stop using Penn to shift the discussion from you, me, and this table." I reached out to rap the sturdy wooden top, and his eyes, somehow, went even rounder.

He stood in a rush, fumbling with his cell phone, then cussing when it hit the floor and bounced under the table. I raised an eyebrow at him when I felt his phone tap my sneaker and land between my feet.

"Could you hand me my phone?" His words were

clipped and icy, but the thick ridge of his dick inside his silken trousers belied all that chill and shade he was throwing.

"No, I don't think so. Why don't you crawl under the table and get it? What you want is right between my legs," I replied, lifting my mug to my lips to take a sip. He was clearly battling internally, but his spine stayed stiff and his knees locked. Several long moments ticked by, his beautiful face shifting from one emotion to another with such speed it was hard to keep track of what I thought he was thinking. Then in a move that stunned me, Mark Westman-Reid went down to his hands and knees. I lost sight of him. My balls grew heavy with anticipation. Would he touch me? Would he not? Would he simply grab his phone and huff off in a fit of pique?

I startled sharply when his hands slid up over my thighs. Coffee lurched out of my cup to my clean white T-shirt with the Raptors logo over the heart. I cussed and swiped at the brown stain, then placed my mug on the table right when his fingers found my fly.

Resting back in my chair, I lowered my sight to the man freeing my cock. I could see only his chin, his wet lips, and the tip of his nose. I needed to see more. I needed to look into his eyes as he sucked me off. His fingers bit into my thighs when I went to push my chair back a bit.

"No, stay there," he said firmly, then nuzzled his soft cheek against my cock. I sucked in a loud breath, grabbed the arms of my chair, and stayed where I was. "If you look at me…"

He didn't finish that statement because he had sucked my cock into his mouth. He sucked hard and fast for a moment, then took a tight hold of me right by the base and moved back to the tip. There he swirled a pink tongue around and around my cockhead, pressing his tongue into the slit, then rubbing his lips up and down both sides.

My head rolled back, and I let loose a long, hot growl that made Mark moan. He licked and nibbled along the shaft, then took me down his throat again. Then he began working me hard, mouth and hand, until I was on the edge of blowing apart. God, but the man knew how to suck dick. His tongue circled over the head time and again, his fingers, tight and slick with spit, pumped unmercifully. I opened my eyes and glanced down to witness his lips stretched around me and his sultry brown eyes resting on my face. I'd slid down a bit it seemed.

I rolled my hips up, to give him more of my cock, and Mark swallowed it all, right down to his fingers. Then he released my dick and took another four or so inches. His thick eyelashes fluttered down, and my balls drew up. My orgasm slammed into me like a Russian enforcer, knocking the wind out of me. Arching and yanking on the arms of the chair, I heard the crack of wood and felt the left arm go lax in my hand. I dropped the broken bit of wood and cushion, then shoved my fingers into Mark's hair to hold him in place as I coated his throat with cum. He gagged and moaned and slid off to breathe, his chin soaked with spittle. A thin line of spunk dangled from his lower lip, and he licked it up, eyes burning into me.

I should probably have said something, but for once, I had no words. I simply lay there sprawled out in that busted chair, panting, my cock pulsing, and stared into his eyes.

He picked his phone up, shimmied out from under the table, used his fancy russet cloth napkin to wipe the spit and cum from his lips, and then walked out of the owners' box pretty as you please in his silky pants and airy summer shirt.

I cleared my throat, tucked my soft dick back into my jeans, and zipped up. Somehow, and I wasn't sure how, but I felt that I'd just had the tables turned on me. And fuck if that sassy exit didn't stir up a deep desire to get all over the man, preferably on the nearest table, and see if I could spin the dynamic back to me being in charge.

Speaking of being in charge, I had a team down on the ice that I was supposed to be watching and making mental notes about.

"Yep, we'll do that just as soon as the rubber legs have gone away," I told the now empty owners' box. Bet my coffee was cold too.

ELEVEN

Mark

_____

OUR FIRST MATCH of the season, an afternoon game, was spectacularly bad.

Letting in three goals in the first period was one thing, but I also had Robert and Clark Lake there, talking Chrysler cars and watching the game with me. I was mortified because how the hell could I sell a winning team to a potential sponsor when said team was losing. I was lost for words, and I could normally talk my way out of most things. Not that Jason was doing any better. The team's new interim general manager was doing a good job of being completely quiet.

"I like that youngster in the net," Robert shared with his brother. "Penn, the one with that cocaine thing."

I groaned internally. The prospects were not good that the two men were linking Colorado with cocaine and not connecting him to being a possible contract for a goalie.

"It's just a tryout," I defended as much as I could without coming out and saying that the coach was messed up and didn't know what the hell he was doing.

Clark shot me a look, "Seriously? You need to lock that

up now. Couple more games and you'll have a powerhouse down there. Add in Madsen and that Alejandro guy, and we're looking at a strong restart to the season." The brothers exchanged looks. "We'd like to see Aarni Lankinen gone, though. He's a liability."

I gave them my patented nod of complete understanding and wished I could wave a magic wand to make that happen. The goal horn sounded, and I stared out at the ice, expecting the scoreboard to show that Vancouver was another goal up.

They weren't. I realized that, even as Robert, Clark, and the entire damn arena rose to their feet and punched the air in unison.

The crowd was chanting, Ry-ker, Ry-ker, and I stood as they replayed the goal. Everything had started right down with Colorado. He'd corralled the puck on a saved shot, passed it to a defenseman who'd shuttled it to another who'd somehow skated through three Vancouver guys, passed to Alejandro, who'd done this impressive stop on the ice, skating back, and blindly passing to Ryker, who'd, and God knows how he did it, managed to swing around the Vancouver goalie and shoot the puck so hard I swore that it left a heat trail. We'd scored.

The crowd was losing their cool below us, dancing and hugging, and I swore, for a moment, the tension in me loosened, and it didn't stop there.

Colorado blocked the next three shots, as easily as if someone was tossing him a tennis ball. Confident and poised, he guarded the net like a dragon with a hoard, and Ryker's line shone like the sun, and when the buzzer sounded at the end of the period, Vancouver hadn't scored again.

By the end of period two, we'd scored twice more, and starting the third we were tied at three goals each. This wasn't how I'd seen this game going. I didn't know hockey, but even I could see that Vancouver seemed edgy, trying for shots when maybe they didn't have a chance, getting into scraps.

"We could win this," Robert said, and he was nearly dancing. In my head, they signed the sponsorship deal right after this match, and it was tantalizingly close.

"What the hell?" Clark asked and stood up close to the glass, his hands flat there.

I didn't even want to look, but I had to. An argument between the Vancouver goalie and one of our forwards morphed into a scuffle, and then a fight where both teams appeared to pair off in some kind of sickening dance. The referees were right in the melee, forcing people apart, and then it became obvious who was at the center of the fight.

Aarni Lankinen. He was shouting when the camera zoomed in, throwing punches that no one seemed to be able to stop, and Vancouver were on him like white on rice. When the crowd of players finally parted, Aarni was given a penalty for instigating and, along with two Vancouver players, was shown to the box. The only thing separating the three of them was the plexiglass between the penalty areas for the Raptors and Vancouver, and Aarni was up, slamming his fist on the glass.

The rest of the game went to shit, and give him his due, Colorado was the main reason we didn't lose by miles. He only allowed in one more goal, but it was enough to secure Vancouver the win, and that was it. Game over.

I shook hands with Robert and Clark, but I could sense that there was an unspoken conversation they wanted to have.

"We're happy to sign…" Robert began, but I didn't celebrate when he looked at his brother and raised an eyebrow.

"But we don't want to be connected to a team who holds on to the past. We want to be part of the new team you promised us," Clark finished the joint thought. Unspoken was the name Aarni, but I knew what they meant. They left after promises to keep in touch, and I sat in the closest seat, staring out over the emptying arena.

Jason sat next to me. "Are they going to sign?" he asked and offered me a beer.

I don't remember ever getting a beer from my big brother. I'd left home before I was legal, but we didn't even sneak underage drinking onto the list of brotherly things to do. I took the bottle but held it and couldn't even bring myself to drink. I was confused about tonight. Colorado had played well; so well that he was first star of the game, with Ryker Madsen and a Vancouver player also being named.

It was weird to think that I'd put Colorado down as a nuisance to be dealt with, and I'd been convinced that Aarni wouldn't be an ass, when tonight I'd been wrong about both of those things. Being wrong was confusing, and knowing I needed to have a conversation with Rowen after I'd avoided him for a few days was acid in my gut.

"They're not signing yet," I said with a sigh. "They're not stupid, and they didn't come outright and say it, but they want to sponsor a team looking to the future. Not one stuck with players on bloated contracts who are a dead weight."

"The legacy contracts," Jason murmured.

"Specifically, Aarni."

Jason shook his head and swallowed the last of his beer. "The problem will still be there tomorrow." He stood and stretched tall. "I need to go. Lewis has a diorama to finish for the science fair, and I promised I'd help. You know, invitation to our place is always there. Hotels can be boring, and I know Lewis would love to show you his project."

I stood and brushed the seat of my pants, leaving the beer on the shelf. "You need to stop doing that, Jason," I warned. "Blackmailing me to visit isn't going to fix anything."

Jason blinked at me, hurt, surprised, but I didn't stay to talk any more. Instead I beat him out of the room and headed to my office to get the list of other potential sponsors. Unfortunately I got caught up answering emails, and then I spent some time catching up with Lucas in New York. By the time I headed for the parking lot, the arena was quiet, and it was easy to hear the shouting before I came around the corner.

"… that wouldn't have happened."

"I know."

"I'm so fucking disappointed in you, and you can see why, right?"

"I'm sorry."

I identified Aarni Lankinen and one of the young players still here on tryouts. Henry, if I'd recalled right. They heard me coming. Aarni drew himself tall and backed away from the other player.

"Mr. Westman-Reid," he acknowledged.

Wide-eyed, Henry looked at me and nodded. There was an air of something happening here, and I didn't like it.

"Everything okay?" I asked casually.

"Yep." Aarni was quick to answer.

Henry more so. "Yes, sir."

I couldn't fail to notice the proprietary hand on Henry's arm and the calculating expression on Aarni's face. What the hell was going on here?

"Goodnight," I said but then waited by my car,

pretending to look at my phone. Aarni and Henry split in different directions, but I made a mental note of what I'd come across and resolved to talk to Rowen about it.

That was, if I could ever face him again after what I'd done. Going to my knees like that, swallowing him down, letting him twist his hands in my hair—what had I been thinking?

Oh, right, I *hadn't* been thinking at all. I shut myself in the car before readjusting myself at the memory of the noises Rowen had made as he was coming. I wanted so much more of that.

More? Like what? A fuck over an office desk?

I could imagine it. I could taste his kisses and feel him thrusting inside of me. I was so hard at the thought of it alone, and it was a while before I was calm enough to drive to the hotel.

It's just sex. Sex is good. You don't have to like someone to have sex with them.

THE KNOCK EARLY the next morning wasn't expected. I hadn't called for room service, nor was I in need of towels. Peering through the hole revealed that it was Jason at my door, and I opened it with a huff of irritation. What was Jason doing here at this time of the day?

"Mark."

It wasn't just Jason standing there, but Cam and Leigh as well, and in front of Cam was Mom.

She looked older, but then, we hadn't seen each other for ten years. Leigh had sent photos every so often, but there was nothing like seeing a person in the flesh to notice the lines. She appeared to be well, despite the cancer, and wore a headscarf that matched her flowing dress and a thick jacket twisted intricately to cover her head.

"Mom," I said but didn't make a move to touch her until, stiffening my spine, I bussed her cheek with a kiss and stood back. She tried to catch and hold me, but I evaded the touch and ignored the hurt in her eyes. What was it with my mom and brothers appearing to be so damned upset all the time? It wasn't me who'd left them. It was *them* who'd thrown me away. I was the one who should feel hurt.

"How are you?" she asked and slid her hand through Jason's arm, looking a little unsteady this close.

"I'm good," I said and then saw Cam sigh.

"Are you going to ask us in?" he asked.

"Not really."

"Mark, please," Leigh said, and I couldn't say no to her, the only one in the family who I owed anything to.

"We should talk," Jason added.

"What do you want to talk about?"

"Jesus, can we do this inside?" Cam snapped and glanced down the empty corridor. There were just two suites on this floor, and I was sure the next one was empty right now. But yeah, a family showdown or intervention or whatever the hell this was had to be done in private. The Westman-Reids didn't do drama in public.

I stepped back from the door and let them in. The suite wasn't big, but it had a separate sitting room and small kitchen and was my home for the near future. I still hadn't gotten myself a real place to live, but then I hadn't *exactly* decided if I was going to stay in Tucson.

"Why are you still in a hotel?" Mom asked. "The house has plenty of bedrooms."

"Yeah, not doing that," I said and rolled my eyes theatrically.

"Your room is still the same," Jason said.

"Sorry, I stopped staring at One Direction posters

when I had to grow the hell up." I was bitter, and every ounce of vitriol was in that statement.

"Fuck's sake," Cam snapped.

I was immediately up in his face. "You have something you want to say?"

Jason pushed between us. "Stop."

"Asshole," I muttered.

"Fuck you," Cam said back.

Mom made a small noise of distress, and Cam was quickly at her side, all his bravado gone in an instant as he guided her to the sofa and fussed over her. She looked pale, and I felt so much guilt I didn't know what to do with the feeling.

"It's probably a good idea to clear the air," Leigh began in the role of mediator.

"He owes me an apology," Cam muttered.

I took the chair opposite Mom, my brothers leaning against the wall, and Leigh by my side.

"Not now, Cam," Leigh warned.

I couldn't let that comment slip by. "No, please explain why you think that I owe *you* an apology, Cam."

He stared at me, and his expression was a run of confusion, then anger, and finally a good side helping of animosity.

"I'll go first," Mom said.

Cam slid down the wall to sit on the floor and shut up, and when Jason did the same, I waited for whatever the hell this was to start.

"Mark, I was wrong, weak, and I should have stopped your dad from cutting you out of our lives. I have no excuse." She coughed, and Cam reached up and pressed a hand to her arm. She sent him a grateful smile and then looked back at me. "He was a dangerous man," she said, and I couldn't fail to see the way she pulled the sleeves of her shirt down on her wrists. "I didn't care for my children the way I should have. I know that, and I hope we can sit down and talk through everything one day because I will always love you." She glanced at Jason and nodded.

"My turn, huh?" He cleared his throat. "I was older than you, and I wanted to find a way to fix everything, and when I couldn't, I was able to retreat to college, and you leaving didn't touch me. I'd even convinced myself that you'd be okay. Then when I checked on you, I wasn't able to see a reason why you'd want any of us in your life. You were happy, successful, you had friends, and I was too ashamed to take that first step. I love you, and I'm so sorry that happened, and Lewis genuinely wants to meet you because I talk about you all the time."

"Uh-huh," I said and saw Jason wince. "And what great words of wisdom do you want to give me, Cam?"

Cam looked up at me with a stormy expression, and for a few moments, the temper that flared in his eyes was hard to see.

"You never told me!" he shouted, then lowered his voice. "You were my best friend, not just my brother, and you never told me who you were or how you felt. I had to find out you were gay when Dad threw you out. Hell, when you left, you didn't care, you didn't look back, and I emailed you, I wrote you fucking letters, for God's sake. I texted you, called you. I even visited you, and you refused to see me? Remember that?"

He rolled to his feet, and I saw his fists were clenched at his sides. Was he expecting me to deny any of it? Actually, I recalled the day with clarity. I'd refused to see him, too wrapped up in my new life, a safe life where people accepted me for who I was. I didn't want the messages or the pleas or the calls or even the damn handwritten notes, when they were just lies.

"You stood next to Dad, and you didn't stop me from leaving." I attempted to talk evenly, but my voice had a crack to it that exposed more than I wanted to show.

"Because I didn't know what was happening. All I knew was that Dad hated you and you'd be better off away from him. From us. And you proved you could be on your own."

"Did you know I slept on the streets for a week? When I got into the city and didn't have any money? Did you care?" I stayed very calm, didn't spit the words at them. In fact, I didn't reveal a single moment of the hurt inside me.

Silence. No one said a word.

"You didn't care, did you, Mom," I said, my heart breaking. It's only what I already knew, but she'd never actually said it to my face before.

"No, I didn't care. Not about you or any of my children," Mom said, tears running down her face, and coughed again, her hand pressed to her chest. "All I cared about was that the shouting would stop. Look." She held out her hands and turned them palm upward, the movement lifting her sleeves. I wasn't close enough to see what she was trying to show me, and then I realized what she must be trying to do. I leaned closer, seeing the scars there, parallel lines running from mid-lower arm to wrist.

"Mom?"

"See, I didn't care about you or anything. I didn't care about Jason, Cameron, or Leigh, so why would you be any different?" She sat straight and had the look of someone waiting for a punishment to be pronounced. A hundred awful thoughts crossed my mind, but I left my seat and crouched in front of her, ignoring my siblings and focusing only on her.

"You wanted to get away that badly?" I asked her gently.

"Your dad... he scared me. He never injured me physically, but he made me doubt myself to the point that I couldn't live for anyone. He threatened all kinds of things after he made you leave, things that let me think it was better for you to leave. Did you know that he wanted to force you into conversion therapy? Mark, he was out of control."

"Shit," Cam muttered.

Mom continued, "I can't make up for all those years when you were on your own, but maybe we could try and talk some more?"

She was begging me. I could see that. I don't remember much about her and Dad's marriage, only that it was very proper and strict in the house. The times I was truly happy was when I was in the gardens with Cam, and I didn't recall Mom as anything but a ghost in her own house.

"We should meet at the house for Sunday dinner?" Jason asked. "All of us should be there, and we can maybe start..." He shrugged as if he'd run out of words. *I know the feeling.*

I met Cam's steely-eyed gaze. Dinner at the house of horrors? With all those memories? I wasn't sure I could handle it.

I gripped Mom's hand, knowing there was a lot to talk through, healing that had to start by opening the wound and letting out the poison.

"Okay," I agreed reluctantly. "Dinner. Sunday. But don't expect me to stay long. I hate that fucking house."

My family left as quietly as they'd arrived, and I sat for the longest time, staring at the walls. Was I wrong to lock them out of my life now? They'd come here and shown nothing but honesty, laid themselves bare to me. Could I move past what had happened all those years ago? The enormity of what they'd just told me, of what Mom had explained, was a heavy weight, and I closed my eyes and remembered the day that Dad had thrown me out.

I remembered crying, from me and my mom, and the harsh words, but they had been from Dad, no one else. I recalled that I was in shock, terrified at what was happening, not knowing where I was going to go, with very little money or hope that any of my friends would take me in.

Their parents were all friends with mine, and none of them would've gone against Dad, because he had so much influence, and at home, he had the last word in everything.

I'd spent so long hating him but just as much time hating my brothers and Mom. I had to learn to trust, but I couldn't get my thoughts in order sitting here with my eyes closed against the world.

I need to get out of here.

The clock showed three p.m. when I left, heading out but not knowing to where until the arena came into view, and that was where I'd been heading all this time. I passed through external security and into parking.

"Hey, Mr. Westman-Reid," Ryker shouted over at me, the man next to him, Alejandro, elbowing him.

I went over to them. "Mark. Call me, Mark. Is Coach Carmichael still inside?"

"Last I saw he was hiding in his office chugging a Dr Pepper," Ryker said.

"Seemed serious," Alejandro added.

"Thanks, guys." I went into the arena, flashing my card and heading straight for the coaches' rooms, not even knocking and walking straight into Rowen's room, closing the door behind me. Rowen leaned back in his chair but didn't say a word. I had to be the one to say something here, the itch of need under my skin, my chest tight, my emotions high.

"I didn't want to like you," I said tiredly.

He shook his head. "Who said I even want you to like me?"

All the emotions of the last few days built, layer on layer, and I was lost for words and not even sure why I was in this damn office, to begin with.

A knock on the door interrupted my spiraling thoughts, and I opened the door. Terri stood there with a folder in her hand. She looked from me to Rowen and narrowed her eyes.

"What's wrong?" she asked.

"Nothing," Rowen said and held out his hand. "Is that the scouting report on the Railers?"

She passed it over and then made sure to stare at me intimidatingly as she walked past me before shutting the door.

I leaned on it to stop any more interruptions, and Rowen crossed his arms over his chest.

"What's wrong?" he asked.

"Everything." I raked a hand through my curls. "Want to get out of here?"

TWELVE

Rowen

_____

To QUOTE AN OLD SAYING, you could have knocked me over with a feather. I'd come to expect a lot of things from Mark Westman-Reid but not him asking me to go somewhere. Him telling me to go somewhere, sure, but an earnest invitation to blow this place at his side? Never in a hundred years. Yet here we were. The invite was on the table, and my curiosity was piqued, to say the least.

"Sure." He seemed oddly pleased about that, which only made this whole episode even more bizarre yet intriguing. "Let me make two calls, and I'll meet you in the parking lot."

He gave me the most peculiar look but inclined his head and sauntered off, his gait that of an utterly defeated man. Curiouser and curiouser…

I rang my mother back, but she wasn't home, off doing tai chi, I wagered. It was her new thing. I left a message, then rang Catalina Foothills Chrysler Plymouth to set up a date for a commercial shoot they'd dangled in front of me. Two commercials in trade for any car from their lot? Uhm, yes, please and thank you. My new agent, Danielle

Turner, from Norwood & Turner Sports and Entertainment in LA, had been ecstatic. NHL coaches with agents was a new niche, but it made sense to have representation. We dealt with multimillion-dollar contracts, and there were endorsement deals to be had, this one with the Lake Brothers being a prime example. She'd helped me wrangle my contract with old man Westman-Reid for prime dollars and total say over coaching staff hirings and firings. With my agent's approval, I was all in for being a Catalina Foothills spokesman. The gorgeous white Chrysler 300 S AWD with dark bronze aluminum wheels, titanium-finish exhaust tips, dark bronze badging, alloy floor mats, black grille with a bronze surround, sunroof, and sound system to make the angels weep, was a sexy bit of cake icing.

I found Mark resting against his Lamborghini with a look of utter rich boy boredom. He wore dark shades and cool desert tones. Gold jewelry to go with his chilly expression. The warm wind tugged on his soft curls.

"We're taking my new car," I said as I walked past him and stopped at my car. His mouth dropped open an inch before he snapped it shut.

"When did you get this?" He ran an appreciative hand over the snow-white fender. "The last I heard you were looking for a car."

"Looks like I found one." I pushed the auto start button on the key fob, and she rolled over with a quick toot of the horn, the AC turned up to maximum blowing away inside. "The Lake brothers have been courting me to do a few TV spots for them."

I caught one sleek brown eyebrow lift over the top of his round sunglasses. "Is this part of the wooing?"

"It is. Obviously I'm a cheap slut. Get in." I opened the driver side door and "Heartache Tonight" blared out of the car. I grinned and winked at Mark, grimacing. "Rock and roll, dude!"

"If you say so," he huffed and slid into his seat, buckling up as the speakers thumped. "Are they the only band you listen to?" he shouted to be heard. I shook my head and tapped the seek button to find another of my favorite bands. "Long Train Running" by the Doobie Brothers assaulted our eardrums.

"I love the bass line in this song. And that harmonica solo? One of the best in rock and roll history, eh?"

"If you say so," he said again.

I laughed at his sour face as we roared out of the parking lot, the sunroof open to let the sweet desert wind circulate around us and play with those damn curls of his. He remained quiet as I took us out of the city. We drove for over an hour, passing several dubious-looking motels and diners until we were in the Sonoran Desert. I pulled off AZ-86 W and killed the engine, silencing the Doobie Brothers.

"Let's go for a walk," I announced, flinging my door open, then grimacing at the heat slapping me in the face. Still, I'd brought us out here to talk, and walking was the best way to get people to talk. Mark eased himself out of the cool luxury of my car. I went to the trunk to fetch a blanket to lay down when he appeared in my peripheral vision.

"You're not serious about walking, are you? This isn't the Mount Lemmon Scenic Byway. It's the desert. There's nothing but rattlesnakes, scorpions, cactus, melanoma, and road runners out here."

"Beep, beep," I teased, slammed the trunk, and took off with the bright blanket under my arm. He followed, his sandals quickly filling with dirt. My sneakers were fine, but holy shit, was it hot. I was saturated in no time. Mark seemed a bit more at ease. "Okay, I'm going to confess that this might not have been such a good idea," I admitted about a quarter of a mile out from the car. Again he gave me that arched eyebrow above the rim of his sunglasses.

"I tried to tell you. If you're going to play in the desert, you have to dress for it. This isn't Ontario. It's Arizona. October strolls in Canada are different than here. You need light-colored loose clothing, a hat, sunglasses, and some sunscreen. Oh, and an antivenom kit at hand." He glanced around our feet. I held my ragged breath to listen for a warning rattle, but I heard none.

"I thought it would be…" *What, Rowen? What exactly did you think it would be? Romantic?* God, no. Not romantic. This thing with Mark had nothing to do with romance. It was sex. Slaking needs. Dirty rutting and sneaky blow jobs. Feelings for Mark need not apply. "Conducive to talking about what's eating you."

He sighed and glanced up at the blistering sun. How could it be in the low nineties in October? *Uhm, because this is a desert, you asshole.*

"My family and I had this intervention thing," he said on a soft whisper that a dry wind tried to carry away. "It was miserable and hopeful."

"Ah, well, that's good, yeah?" I knew little about the Westman-Reid family dynamic other than what I'd witnessed. The other brothers struck me as big douches, but his sister was a delight. I'd not met the matriarch yet. Probably I would next week at the Desert Nights Cancer Charity event the team was sponsoring at some swanky hotel. All Raptor players and coaching staff were to attend in evening wear. The thought of rubbing elbows with aristocrats made me twitch.

He bobbed his head, his brow dewy with sweat. Mine was coated. Sweat ran into my eyes, down my neck, and into the crack of my ass. Canadian boys in the desert sun grew miserable quickly. What had I been thinking?

You were thinking of finding some oasis and spreading Mark out over that knock-off Navajo blanket and getting to know his body much, much better.

Okay, yeah, that might have been a small nugget of a plan when we'd set out but—

"… turned their backs on me. How am I supposed to just overlook years of loneliness?"

I stared at the man staring at me. "I grew up next door to my cousin. Thick as thieves we were, played hockey together, got into trouble together. When he found out I was gay, he pulled away from me, and we never spoke again. One day he called, but I was too angry to pick up, my hurt was too engulfing to let me take the olive branch. I never called him back. During his senior year at college, he was in a car accident and died. It was… pretty horrible. I was devastated and eaten up with guilt. I should have swallowed my pride. I should have taken his call. There was no way to go back then. We don't get rewinds. If your family is trying to bridge the past, then at least meet them halfway."

A long silence shrouded us. "That's the first time I've ever heard you talk about something personal."

I shrugged, the back of my neck incredibly hot and tingly. "I'm not here to talk about my life. I'm here to coach your hockey team."

"Are you seeing anyone?"

I blinked at the salt in my eyes and the directness of his question. "If I were dating someone, I would not have allowed things to happen between us. What kind of man do you think I am?"

"I have no idea what kind of man you are aside from what I read online. You're incredibly closed off and private. There's no mention of you being gay anywhere on the internet."

"Who I take to my bed is no one's business," I was quick to reply.

"Okay, that's fair. So what is this then?" He waved a hand to me, then patted his chest. "What are we doing here?"

"We're having sex. Why does it have to be more than that? We really don't even like each other all that much, but there *is* an overwhelming animal attraction that keeps us circling each other like horny goats." He wet his lips, and I knew I had him. Or I was pretty sure I had him. He might have just been thirsty because holy fucking hell, the desert was *hot*. I took a few steps closer so that I could inhale the aroma of his sweat mingling with his pricey cologne. My dick began to fatten up as soon as I smelled that sweet, sexy scent. "We can do this one of four ways. We can have sex in the back of the car, we can have sex out on the ground, we can have sex on the hood of the car, or we can go back to that seedy motel we passed, the Gila Monster Motor Court, and have sex in a dingy room. I'll let you decide, but please note that every scenario ends with me pounding you like a mallard duck."

"I just… a duck?"

"*South Park* reference. Not important."

A twisted little smile played on his lips. "Seedy hotels seem to be our thing…"

Oh yes, I fucking had him. We ran back to the car, dived in, and hightailed it to the Gila Monster Motor Court. Check-in was easy and frightfully cheap. Two hours for forty bucks. As we walked to our room, I checked out the cars in the parking lot. There were a lot of them. I suspected that we'd stumbled into a hooker haven. Room ten was stuffy, poorly lit, and had a bed. A big bed. No dresser. The air conditioning was mediocre. The room smelled of old cigars, bad whiskey, and cheap perfume. It was perfect.

Mark was horrified, I could tell, so I anchored his back to the door, leaned my body into his, and kissed that grimace of disgust off his sensual lips. He responded like a man possessed. Fingers grasping handfuls of hair, hips rolling, tongue wrapping and gliding over mine. The man made me nuts and not all in a bad way. I needed to taste him. All of him, so I began yanking on his clothing. He moaned and whined into my mouth as buttons flew and belts were tossed to the wall. His need was as wild as mine, and soon we were naked, weeping cocks pressed together, my hands on his tight little ass. We danced to the bed, and I fell over him, locking my lips to his as I nudged his thighs apart. He hit the mattress, and his legs fell wide open.

"Oh, fuck, this bed..." he huffed as I tongued a brown nipple. "I can't... this bed is probably covered with..."

"Don't think about it," I panted, then took his nipple between my teeth. He gasped, groaned, and gyrated.

"I can't *not* think about it."

I reached down between us, balancing on one arm, and found his hole. His spine arched like a handcrafted bow as I pressed a dry finger against his ass.

"Think about me taking this ass of yours."

"Yes, mm, fuck, yes," he whimpered, clawing at the questionable bedding, all worries about the cover being clean or dirty was now gone, it seemed. "Fuck me, fuck me, fuck me."

"Roll over." I didn't need to be told—or begged—twice. He flipped over with haste. Resting on his elbows, he offered me his ass wantonly, moving back and forth as if teasing a hungry dog with a bone. I spat on my finger, then pressed it into his ass, bending over to bite his left buttock.

The man began speaking in tongues. More spit, more fingers, more nips and suckle marks on his ass cheeks got him so wound up he could barely put two words together.

"Fuck me!"

Guess I was wrong. He could put two words together. I removed my fingers and tongued his hole, lying belly down on the ugly floral bedspread. Hands spreading him wide, I speared his hole over and over, then moved down to his balls and sucked them with vigor. His cock dangled down in front of me, slick with precum, so I grabbed it and pulled it back to my lips.

"Ah... fuck... me... shit... hurry," Mark cried out, reduced now to merely shouting single words to express himself. Popping off his lovely cock, I then slid off the bed, found my pants and wallet, and hurried back to him. "Christ, I'm so close," he mewled as I rolled a condom down over my dick, then ripped open the lube packet with my teeth.

"Don't you come yet. I want you to come when I'm inside you, not before."

"Mmmm Mmmm." He hummed as his ass moved in a side to side motion. I doused his spittle-coated hole with lube, then worked it slowly into him, using my fingers to rub and coat him internally. When he was slicked up and muttering vowels only, I took his hips in my hands and pulled him back onto me, inch by inch, giving him a second to adjust to my possession. God above but he was hot and tight. I bent down over his back, nipped at his shoulder, then leaned back and pumped into him with a passion. He yelped when I drove home, my fingers deep into his flesh, keeping him still as I reveled in the feel of his body stretching around me, accepting me, and then gently constricting around me.

"Ah… Oh… more. More. Ahh, god… more! Fuck me harder. Rowen, oh shit, that's… yes!"

He was shouting now. A more vocal, beautiful bottom I'd never had the pleasure of being with. The man was wildly passionate, his cries and shouts spurring me on. I gave him harder and faster, pounding into him with such force that he was now resting against the headboard, his fingers digging at and shredding the worn wallpaper over the bed. Someone in the next room shouted at us to be quiet, so I fucked Mark harder. He pounded on the wall, his brow resting on the headboard. My balls tightened up, and I thrust one final time, as deep as I could go. A low, keening sound escaped him. I fumbled around under him, finding his cock. He fucked my hand for a moment, then shot all over the pillows and sheets. I wiped my fingers on his throat and jawline, then jerked him upright and licked off the thick, warm lines of his cum from his overheated skin. He was salty and musky, a wonderful taste. I went back for more, cleaning off his neck and jaw. Mark sagged in my arms, spent and coated with sweat. We tumbled to our sides, my cock slipping free of his ass. He made a sad little sound at the loss.

I peppered his chin and eyelids with kisses, easing him closer to my side. I felt something soaking through my hair to dampen my scalp.

"I think I'm lying on your cum puddle," I informed him. He snorted weakly as he battled to catch his breath. I was too satisfied to care overly much. "You're a wild little bottom, aren't you?" I rolled my head so that I could enjoy his profile.

"Sometimes," he confessed, rolling to the side to look at me. "Do you always top?"

"Mm, usually. You okay with that?"

"Yeah, I am." He pushed up to rest on his elbow, his hand bolstering his head. "Can we do this again?"

"Give me ten minutes or so. A little water would be nice." I gave him a wink, then left the bed, padding into the bathroom and flushing the condom. As much as I needed a shower, the scummy residue on the shower door gave me second thoughts. The cum drying on my hair overran my worries about soap scum, and I jumped in, using a small bar of soap to wash both my body and my hair because someone had not stocked any shampoo. The towel smelled a little funky when I dried my face. I found a small tube of toothpaste that I prayed had been put there by the management, and brushed my teeth with my index finger. Tying the towel around my waist, I walked back to the room, finding Mark seated on the bed, wonderfully naked yet, his legs stretched out in front of him, nursing a cold bottle of water. "Where did you get that?"

"The machine outside."

I tossed the towel to the floor and crawled into bed with him. We still had an hour to kill. "Did you dash out with your balls bouncing in the wind?"

"No, I pulled my pants on. Then I took them off because I thought I might want you again." He passed me the bottle, his brown eyes making all kinds of carnal promises I hoped his hands, mouth, and ass were planning on keeping. "Do you do this often? Hook up in questionable motels with men you don't like?"

I drank most of the water, handed it back to him, and then ran a finger down his still tacky chest. He had a fine line of hair running between his pectorals down over his flat stomach, then ending in a neatly trimmed bush of dark curls.

"Not really. I don't really date much."

"Too busy with hockey?" He finished the bottle, then tossed it to the floor beside the wet towel.

"No, too busy not caring about it."

His eyebrow danced up his forehead and got lost in damp curls. How cute. "Are you recovering from a broken heart?"

I cupped his chin, hoping he'd stop the inquisition, and led his mouth to mine. He opened with eagerness, leaning up and into the kiss, his arms slowly coming around my neck. I took him down to the bed, sliding a leg between his and licking into his mouth with lazy passion.

"Tell me." He sighed when my lips traveled down his throat. "Tell me why you don't date. Are you snakebit?"

I paused in my seduction, lifting my head up from the joy that was his clavicle. "Can we shelve this for a later time. We have less than fifty minutes now, and I can think of much better ways to spend that time than rehashing old romances that went down in flames."

"So you're so averse to romance because you were hurt. See, that makes—where are you going?" He sat up when I left the bed to find my pants. "I didn't mean to open up any wounds that might not be healed. I just want to know more about you."

I stepped into my underwear, then yanked my jeans up over my ass with attitude. "All you need to know about me is what I put on my résumé."

"You never filled out a résumé. You signed a contract that was negotiated with my father and you and an agent who I suspect used her wiles on my father to get you some of the most outrageous provisos I have ever seen included in an NHL coach's contract." He threw himself off the bed as he barked at me. "What do you really know about hockey coaching contracts? Or hockey for that matter?"

"I know enough to see that yours is going to be the

death of this club," he snapped back. Oh my, I did love seeing that fire in his eyes. Such a sexy man he was when his dander was up. Speaking of up, my dick was getting nice and hard now. I unzipped, shoved my pants and underwear down to my ankles, and took my cock in hand. Mark's gaze flew down to my dick, and he ran the tip of his tongue over his lower lip.

"Forty minutes now," I said, and he nodded, his eyes roaming over my chest, then slowly closing as he crawled back into the bed, lay down on his back, and reached between his legs to play with his glistening, slicked-up hole. I fell on him, ravenous, claiming his mouth and his ass again in bed and then once more in the shower, which he used but only under extreme duress.

We were an hour late checking out. I grabbed a book of matches and tossed them to Mark as we walked to my car. "Call them when we get home. Set up a weekly rendezvous time for us. And next time make sure you bring lots of condoms, lube, and toys."

He gave me a dour look, but I knew he'd call. "When you say toys, do you mean rope?"

Now it was time for me to raise an eyebrow. "Do you *want* it to mean rope?"

He smiled that devil's smile and got into the car. I grinned at the sun slowly sinking in a beautiful purple and pink desert skyline. I suspected that this man was going to keep me on my toes. I couldn't wait to return to the Gila Monster Motor Court next week to see what kind of dance he'd lead me through next.

THIRTEEN

Mark

I DIDN'T LIKE to be laughed at. I was used to it, but I didn't have to like it.

In New York, everyone had laughed at the newbie model who wanted to go it alone. In my family I was always the youngest, the baby and fodder for everyone's jokes. Also, I was sure out there in Hockey-land the fact that a former model being part of a team attempting to drag the Raptors into order was enough to cause all kinds of hilarity.

So yeah, I had thick skin that not much penetrates, but what I'd just come across was enough to have me seeing red.

"You can go," I told Henry.

Aarni took one look at me and smirked before turning his attention back to Henry. "You can stay."

"Henry…" I warned and stared until he realized who he should be listening to.

Henry extricated himself from where Aarni had him blocked in a corner, and hurried as fast as he could on skates with the guards on, back toward the locker room without a backward glance. Aarni turned to face me fully, propped up on the wall, smug as shit.

"Can I help you, Mr. Westman-Reid?"

"You want to repeat what you just said?" I asked and crossed my arms over my chest. I was already shorter than Aarni, add in the fact that he was on skates and he towered over me.

He tilted his head as if he was examining me, and he still had that smug grin on his face.

"What part?" he asked.

"The part about Mark, the pansy-ass pretty boy who thinks he can call the shots when he's a waste of fucking space?"

Oh yeah. I'd heard the whole thing or at least the last of whatever poison Aarni was pouring into Henry's ears. I wasn't even supposed to be down here, but when I'd received an email with yet another coaching change from Rowen, you'd better believe I'd worked up a head of steam and was heading straight for his office. Which is when I took a wrong freaking turn in this maze of corridors, which took me right through the locker room, much to my embarrassment, and then out the other side to whatever *this* was.

I waited for Aarni to be embarrassed, mortified, apologetic, but he laughed in my face, then pushed himself from the wall and mirrored my stance. He was daring me to say more, and a small prick of uncertainty had me wavering a little. He was intimidating and laughing at me, and I felt like a stupid little kid. Then he leaned in closer and whispered.

"Maybe you and me could get some time at Gila Monster Motor Court, huh?"

The bottom fell out of my world, and my shock must

have been visible because he winked at me and then crowded me back, much as he had Henry.

"Step away," I managed, but he didn't do as I asked. Instead he stared down at me. I could smell his cloying aftershave up this close and see the derision in his eyes. He didn't respect me; he didn't respect the team. I doubt that he respected anyone but himself.

"Mr. Westman-Reid?" A voice from behind us had Aarni moving away smoothly, to reveal Ryker Madsen. "Henry just came in looking weird. Everything okay?" he added.

Aarni smiled at me, but the smile didn't reach his eyes and with the animosity in his gaze, I couldn't help but feel threatened.

"Management stuff," Aarni said dismissively and stalked past Ryker, brushing the younger man's arm with enough force that Ryker had to steady himself on his skates. For a second Ryker tensed, and I waited for a smackdown between the two, but then Ryker shook it off.

"You okay, sir?" he asked again with the greatest respect.

I nodded because that was about the limit of communication right now, and Ryker frowned.

"You want me to get someone?"

I shook my head mutely, then pulled my shoulders back. What was I going to say? That right about now I felt like an idiot, and a big part of me wanted Ryker to fetch Rowen so that he could calm me the hell down.

"Everything's okay," I said and pasted as confident a smile as I could manage on my face. It must have been convincing because Ryker headed back to the locker room, only stopping just outside the door and turning to face me.

"Aarni's not worth it," Ryker murmured. "You should watch him, sir."

"Thank you, I will."

Since when was advice from someone fresh into their twenties so insightful? I continued on to Rowen's office, but he wasn't in there. I found him waiting on the ice, and I knew I couldn't interrupt him as the team headed out for a game-day training session. He didn't even look my way, and I was restless and angry and ashamed at not being able to handle Aarni's shit.

When Aarni skated by and winked at me through the plexiglass, I turned tail and fled back to my office like an idiot.

"What happened?" Jason asked as I passed him by the coffee machine in the management complex. He looked exhausted, but then he was juggling being interim general manager of the team with his own work for the Westman-Reid foundation.

"What?" I tried for innocent, but Jason got that big brother expression on his face. With a sigh, I admitted to myself that I needed to talk to someone. "Can we talk?"

"In there." He pointed at his office, and I slipped in, and it felt right to want to talk to him, and maybe I needed some big brother wisdom. He followed me in, passed me a coffee of my own, then shut the door with his heel. "You look like you've seen a ghost."

How much did I tell him? How about the fact that I was sleeping with the head coach or that actually it was less sleeping and more fucking each other into oblivion. We'd just passed week three, and I'd yet to take ropes or toys or anything with me to our hookups that wasn't vanilla.

Not that what we did was vanilla, and I squirmed in my seat at the memory of the last time. Me, over the bed, unable to move, and Rowen explaining what he was doing to me in such exquisite detail as he fucked me hard…

Nope, I wasn't going to tell Jason about what his little

brother was getting up to in a no-tell motel with dirty ceilings. Which meant how could I begin to explain Aarni and his intimidation techniques? I sipped the coffee, the caffeine delicious and much needed. Drinking gave me a few moments to think, and by the time I was halfway through the cup, I was ready to talk.

"We need to check the Aarni contract again."

There, that was easy enough. No mention of rough-and-ready sex, or the fact that I thought Aarni had threatened me with revealing what he knew, or questions as to how the hell he knew at all.

Jason sat back in his chair, reaching down for a folder and placing it on his desk.

"A cap hit of four million for each of the two years remaining on his solid gold no-move contract. Which means Aarni can't be traded or sent to the minors without his permission. The only way out as GM, is to buy out his contract and then place him on waivers without permission. He won't go for it, and we don't have the money to do it. That is our *only* out."

"Eight million." I exhaled noisily because that was insurmountable for the Raptors right now. With falling ticket revenue, lack of sponsorship and investment, and a failing team, we didn't have eight thousand to waste, let alone eight million.

"Not that it will be that up front, but it could cost us big-time, stop the team from having the money to spend on someone good to fill his spot." He scrubbed his eyes. "I've checked the rules—we have to multiply the remaining salary by the buyout amount, which is all dependent on age, and that gives us the total buyout cost, which we can spread evenly over twice the remaining contract years, so that's four years." He checked the piece of paper on his desk. "Something about subtracting the annual buyout cost by the player's salary, which gives us a cap hit, which you then take off annual average salary. I don't fucking know what I'm talking about."

"What the hell was Dad thinking?"

"You really want to go there?" Jason asked and joined me in a sigh. "And he doesn't even have a morals clause in his contract. But then, that would be ineffective anyway. Believe me, I had the lawyers at Westman-Reid check every detail. They told me that hockey is a game where violence and intimidation on ice wasn't something that would trigger a clause anyway, so Dad didn't have one put in."

I sunk into the soft chair and rested my coffee on my belly. Something in what Jason had said made me think. "What about a crime? What if he assaulted someone or threatened assault?"

Jason straightened in his chair and very deliberately placed his coffee on a coaster emblazoned with the Raptors logo. "Did he threaten you?" he asked. "Is that what got you so rattled?"

"No, but he…" I paused and checked behind me to make sure the door was shut. "I think he has a weird kind of coercive control over Henry." I didn't add that I'd just had a taste of the same shit and had very nearly crumbled. Aarni was a big, threatening presence, and there was a scary hate in his expression. God knows what his anger and pressure did to the younger guys on the team.

"You *think*? Do you have actual proof?" Jason picked up a pen, and I thought he expected me to detail what I knew. Which was nothing but what I instinctively *thought*.

"I don't have anything explicit."

Jason put the pen down, but he didn't seem angry, just disappointed. "Maybe Coach Carmichael can pull Aarni around, and we're worrying about nothing?"

I thought Rowen wanted to kill the guy, not pull him around, which led me to the next issue I needed to tell my GM, or my brother, or in whatever capacity Jason needed to know.

"Rowen and I have been seeing each other."

Jason raised his eyebrows. "Define 'seeing.'"

Hot, sweaty, desperate sex, in the dirtiest, nastiest way, very often three times in one visit, and oh yeah, I'm addicted, and I don't think I hate him anymore, and actually I might like him a bit.

"Seeing," I repeated meaningfully and added a nod, which appeared to allow Jason to understand.

"Well, uhm. Okay," Jason murmured and picked up his pen again, tapping it on the Aarni Lankinen folder. "Stay safe and… yeah." He looked embarrassed, and I decided to let him off the hook.

"It's okay, big brother. I wasn't asking for permission or needing guidance. I just thought as GM you should know."

He blustered a bit and then gave me a rueful sigh. "Just be careful, and I don't mean in a condom kind of way. Shit"—he scrubbed at his eyes—"I didn't need to add that, did I?"

"Not really," I agreed and then grinned at him. How was it that this brotherly stuff was enough to make me smile? Go figure.

Jason changed the subject. "You're still coming tomorrow, right?"

"Sunday dinner at the house of horrors to meet my nephew properly and to be asked all kinds of awkward questions and sit with Cam and pretend not to be pissed at him. Yes."

"About Cam, I'd love it if you cut him some slack," Jason said in all seriousness. "When you left, it broke his heart, and then you blocked him from your life."

I stood, angrily. "Jesus—"

"No, wait, don't go. I get why it all went down that way. I know you were protecting yourself. I know you hated us, just… he's your brother, and he loves you. If you love him back at all, then maybe let that show a bit? For me? Please?"

I wanted to be angry, but there wasn't anger there, just a quiet resolution that maybe I did need to find a common ground with my family. After all, Dad was gone now, and dinner was a start.

"Okay."

"If you want to, you can bring Coach Carmichael as your date."

I snorted a laugh. "It's not *that* kind of thing we have going on."

It was only when I got into my own office that I realized one big thing. I kind of wished Rowen could come with me for dinner at my parents' house. Not like boyfriends, but because he was a man who seemed to be on my side.

And I needed that.

I STAYED at the arena for the night's game. Florida were in town, and management had already been given a heads-up that this meant Tennant Rowe's brother was in the barn. Matchups with the Rowe brothers, one in Florida and the other brother in Boston, were always heated. Mainly because of the fact that Aarni Lankinen had nearly killed their little brother. Half the fans here, in Florida colors, wanted a clean, exciting game, and the other half, in Raptors gold, wanted Aarni to take the Rowe brother from Florida down. They wanted blood, and some of the signs at the glass were evil, talking about the gay shit and the fact that the Rowe family were infected. They made me feel sick, and I wasn't sure whose responsibility it was to instruct them to be taken down. Was it us? Should we be doing something about this?

I peered down from my lofty position, seeing the two teams out on the ice for warm-ups, and no sign of Rowen yet. There was unrest in the crowd, booing, but I couldn't see why.

"Coach made Lankinen a healthy scratch, apparently," Jason said and pocketed his cell.

"Which means what?" I asked as the volume of boos grew louder.

"Means he's healthy and fit to play, but that Coach has benched him."

I leaned out and tried to make out who was playing on our team, but the only names I could make out were ones where there were close-ups on the huge video screen in front of me. No Lankinen.

"Can he do that?"

"Yes, I can," Rowen said from the door, and I turned to face him. He had a thunderous expression on his handsome face, and his hands were clenched in fists at his side. He glared at the others in the box. "I need the room cleared," he said. And everyone except Jason and I left without argument. I stayed because I thought it was me who he really wanted to talk to, and Jason because hell, he clearly got the stubborn Westman-Reid genes, and he was also the GM. He stood with his arms crossed over his chest, defying Rowen to tell him to leave. Seemed to me he was trying for protective, and it was nice. Rowen slammed the door after the last person left, then pulled the blinds.

"My greatest weapon is my ability to control players' ice time," he began and leaned against the door. "Sitting out that underperforming fucktard of a millionaire could be the perfect way to get him to rethink blackmailing his fucking coach."

"What?" Jason said and looked from me to Rowen and back again.

"Asshole says he's happy to keep my *liaison* with one of the Westman-Reids to himself. He didn't express terms, but I believe the implication of sharing said Westman-Reid with him was the icing on that particular fucked-up cake."

All my energy left me, and I sank to the chair.

Jason cleared his throat. "What the hell?"

"Exactly," Rowen said. Something passed between my brother and my lover, and when both of them stared at me, I knew they were both in protecting-Mark mode, and I didn't even have the energy to bristle with indignation.

"Okay," Jason began after their silent communication. "Back to how this affects the team. You know how this will look to the journalists, to the rest of the team."

Rowen tensed. "What? You don't think the team will bounce back from me being in a relationship with your little brother?"

"No, I mean, yes. I mean. Shit." Jason massaged his temples. "I'm happy for the two of you. That isn't my concern. It's just we're exposed already with the money riding on him, and becoming a healthy scratch could signal that he's on the downside of his career. It could spark all kinds of questions about a player's future. Fans might think we're trying to trade him or that his career is in jeopardy. How the hell is the team going to deal with his big-money contract while he's benched?" Now it was Jason's turn to sit down.

I'd listened to everything Jason said, but I couldn't get away from the fact that Rowen used the term *relationship*. Is that what he thought we had going here?

The door pushed behind Rowen, and he stepped out

of the way, the people who had left now returning, and along with them, a furious-looking Aarni Lankinen, who shouldered his way to a far seat and sat mutinously. He wasn't dressed for hockey. In fact he was still in his suit. The team box was clearly where healthy scratch players sat.

"Fucking smile," Rowen ordered him, and Aarni gave a half grimace that would have to do. I exchanged looks with Jason. How was this going to appear up on the screen? Rowen turned to leave.

"Coach Carmichael? The signs on the glass, we've seen some of them on the video screen. Can we get them removed? Who do we ask?"

Rowen nodded. "Security. I'm on it."

After he left, I swiveled the luxurious chair and stared down at the glass where the signs were. It didn't take long for security to reach them, and a couple of the holders didn't go quietly. The ones that backed down were allowed to stay; the others ejected.

When the game itself started, it was obvious we were on the defensive. In goal, Colorado was like a brick wall, steadier in his role than I had seen him before. Our fast guys at the front managed to get two goals past the Florida goalie, but it was four penalties drawn on our team, resulting in power plays, which had us eventually losing by two. What became more obvious as I watched was that the fans for our team were negative, booing, and with a palpable air of resentment. They didn't respect the team, and I doubt the team was that happy hearing the noise they made. We needed to fix that. Aarni left the room as soon as the game ended, and I headed out after him to find Rowen. I stood right at the back of the room as Rowen took his place in the Coach's Corner postgame review, waiting for questions from the assembled journalists. I couldn't believe that for a team in such dire straits there were so many of them here.

"Coach? Guy Stevens. Zona Hockey."

"Hello, Guy."

"Can you explain why you made Aarni Lankinen a healthy scratch tonight?" Murmurs spread as the elephant in the room was addressed.

I held my breath, waiting for Rowen to spill his guts about respect and blackmail and a hundred other things we didn't want him to say. He leaned toward the microphone.

"He was late for practice," Rowen lied and gave a what-can-I-tell-ya shrug.

The journalist pressed for more. "Do you think that if Lankinen had been in the lineup you would have won tonight?"

Rowen lifted a single eyebrow. "We'll never know."

"Is this a punishment that fits the crime, Coach?" someone else asked.

"Respect is key in this team."

And that was clearly all he was going to say. The rest of the interview was him talking about prospects and playing the game and the team buying into the process. Nothing more than sound bites.

I followed him out of the room, at a distance, all the way to his office, and slipped inside the door. He looked at me warily, and a hundred different things passed between us.

I cleared my throat. "Will you come to dinner at my family's place tomorrow?"

"Really?"

I died inside and was sorry I'd even asked, because he didn't exactly jump all over the idea, and mostly looked as if he was in shock. Then he softened a little and I felt like I could explain my question.

"Just as a friend, if that's what you want," I blurted.

He paused a moment. "What if we went as a couple? You know, as people who dated?" His question threw me.

"Is that what we are doing? Dating?"

He hesitated for a moment, then nodded. "I think we are."

"I like the sound of that," I admitted.

He smiled at me. "Yeah. Me too."

FOURTEEN

Rowen

_____

"So, did we make a wrong turn at Albuquerque?" I inquired on the sly as Mark and I made our way into the Westman-Reid dining room. He gave me his classically prince-like look of utter confusion. "To quote Bugs Bunny —you do know who he is, right—or did you only watch Richie Rich cartoons growing up?"

"No. Sadly, Richie Rich wasn't quite greedy enough. We were all made to sit at the television in our prep school uniforms and study _Duck Tales_ so that we could, someday, the gods of Wall Street willing, grow up and emulate Scrooge McDuck."

I had to smile at the man. He was horrendously sharp-witted, with just the right amount of disdain to his biting comments. If there was one thing that made me hot, it was a man I could verbally spar with. Mark, aside from being one flaming hot whirlwind of a bottom in bed, was one of the sauciest and classiest comeback kings I'd ever had the fortune of fucking.

Servants hustled around, pulling out chairs and smiling that bland domestic help smiled. I'd not felt quite at home in this massive testament to corporate greed when I'd been here before, and this trip wasn't endearing the Westman-Reid mansion to me. His family, on the other hand, was damned engaging for the most part. The kids were cute, as kids went. They were normal kids and not overly pretentious. Two wives who smiled and shook my hand but whose names I forgot as soon as they'd been given to me. Lovely women who had made lovely children who would keep the Westman-Reid name and bloodline rolling along nicely.

I'd come to grudgingly respect Jason now that he'd taken on the thankless mantle of GM for the team. Cameron was still an insufferable anal fissure, but Leigh was a sheer delight.

We took our seats. I was to sit beside Mark on one side of a massive dining table that seated perhaps forty people. My gaze traveled over the gold flatware, fine china, and huge bouquet of white and pink flowers. Not sure what kind of flowers they were. I knew hockey, not floral arranging, but they had no aroma at all. Maybe they were fake. Kind of like this whole damn dinner thing.

I ran a finger over the perfectly aligned flatware as we all stood waiting for the matriarch to appear.

"So, do the staff measure the silverware placement with a ruler like they do at Buckingham Palace?" I asked whoever might deign to reply. Cameron glowered at me. Leigh giggled behind her hand. Jason snorted, and Mark rolled his eyes. "If you'd have told me this was a state dinner, I would have dressed better."

Mark's gaze roamed over my *Eagles-On the Border* T-shirt, black jeans, well-worn sandals, and a denim jacket ensemble. Everyone else was uptown chic casual or whatever the hell fashionable name could be applied.

"It's just dinner, nothing fancy, but Mom likes to see us

put a little effort into dressing well for the evening meal," Leigh finally replied as she wheeled herself closer to the table, then shook out a cloth napkin and laid it over her lap. "I wore a halter top and a kilt to dinner last week." She gave me a wink that I returned.

"You also got dark looks all through the quail," Jason parried.

Mark was about to chime in when Mrs. Westman-Reid showed up. She was a stately woman, dressed in silky slacks and a sharply pressed blouse. Hair and makeup on point, as the kids said, and small pearls in her ears and around her long neck. Elegant and poised, she smiled at us all, pecking the grandkids on the cheek before taking her seat at the head of the table. A spot, I was sure, the patriarch had once planted his ass in.

"You're looking wonderful, Mother," Cameron said as we all sat. Appetizers were served immediately, water goblets were filled, and Mark began talking about some vague little thing he'd seen on the Internet. Being a simple boy from Canada, I poked at the white square resting on a small china plate.

"Uhm," I said, and all eyes rolled in my direction. "Not to sound uncouth, but what the hell is this?" I tapped the white square with a tine.

"It's daikon radish box with a dollop of crab salad on top," Mark explained, his knee coming to rest on mine in a comforting way that I enjoyed.

"Ah yes, I should have recognized it right off. We served this all the time at home, right before the poutine course."

Leigh and the kids found that hilarious, and even Mark and Jason snuffled in amusement.

"It's so nice to have someone here from another country," Mrs. Westman-Reid said between nibbles on her radish block. "What kind of foods do you enjoy when you return home to Ontario? It is Ontario where you hail from, isn't it, Coach Carmichael?"

"Mom, he's from *Canada*. That really doesn't count as a major foreign country. Not like he's from France, England, or any of the other elite European countries." Cameron tossed that out glibly.

Being a proud Canuck, I took instant offense, but Mark's hand on my knee under the table stilled my tongue. Or not. I pushed my radish block to Mark after I scraped off the crab meat and ate it. "Please, ma'am, call me Rowen. And yes, I am from Ontario. We have some marvelous foods in Canada, aside from poutine, which I just mentioned. We enjoy butter tarts, Jiggs dinner, tourtiere, Nanaimo bars, beavertails, ketchup chips, barbequed ribs, sugar pies, and of course real maple syrup, and the best bacon anywhere."

"That all sounds delicious. I've always wanted to see Canada, but I do fear the moose. They have such rubbery faces. Have you had many moose encounters, Rowen?"

"Mother, I'm pretty sure that moose don't ramble around Toronto or Ottawa on a daily basis," Jason said, then deftly moved the conversation to non-moose topics.

I could have told them that we did see moose on occasion in the big cities, but I decided to let the topic go. The grandkids were vocal during the meal, and the conversation was smooth, if not a little vapid. No one really touched on anything meaty, just general dinnertime talk followed with coffee or sherry and dessert. I'd kind of been hoping to talk with the men about the Aarni situation, but it seemed we weren't going to be afforded the time for business talk.

After the meal, Mark and I slipped out of the rear door of the solarium and snuck off to the pool house where I took several liberties with him. When I had him sweaty, sated, and spent in my arms, I kissed him gently for the longest time, the brilliant Arizona sun now well settled in the West. His body was flushed and warm from passion. I tucked him back in, zipped his pants, and ran my fingers over his lips, enjoying the puffiness from all my kisses.

"Did you like that?" I inquired as I held him to the wall with just my body weight, the tang of his cum still on my tongue.

"God, yes." He sighed, pushing his fingers into my hair. "So, are we now done with the Gila Monster Motor Court?"

"Fuck that and fuck Aarni. I don't allow anyone to dictate my life," I snarled, the rush of sneaking in a quick blow job to pleasure my lover on the grounds of the Westman-Reid estate disappearing at the mention of that bastard Lankinen. "I also do not bow down to blackmailers. I'm not sure how he found out about us, nor do I care. That room is ours, our little escape from the chaos of life, and that pig-faced jerk is not taking that away from us."

He wet his lips. I stole another kiss, then yet another. There was no way in hell I was giving Mark up. The sex was incredible, and I'd come to enjoy the time we spent after the act as well, him stretched out over me, talking about the trials and tribulations of life as our overheated bodies cooled. It was just what I wanted. Sex and someone to talk to. No strings attached. No chance of being crucified by a man with a pretty face again. Losing Mark… him… it… would be a loss I was not willing to contemplate. I prayed the team lawyers or someone in the gilded boxes way above where I spent my time could come up with a solution. It was the end of October, and we'd only managed to scrape together a handful of wins. There were many reasons for that, not just Aarni, but his particular brand of toxicity was not helping. We needed to purge his poison from the locker room before we could hope to see healing begin.

Mark pulled me down for another lengthy kiss, the rasp of his tongue over mine pushing hockey from my mind for a tiny bit, and for that, I thanked him by holding him as close as possible and kissing him back until he was breathless and wanting yet again. We made the run out to the Gila Monster Motor Court in record time that night.

THIS WAS NOT the holiday gift that a hockey coach wanted. Nope, not at all. I ran my fingers through my hair, looked up at the clock, and grimaced. Had we *really* only played fifteen minutes of hockey? Had the Railers honestly scored on Colorado four times in those fifteen minutes? Had Santa forsaken me? Thank Christ, Harrisburg made this west coast sweep only once a year. We wouldn't have to face them until late April when we made a sprint up the East coast. Maybe by April, the severe ass-reaming without even the courtesy of lube or a reach-around we were getting would be a distant memory. A man could hope.

"We have *got* to tighten up in the offensive zone!" Terri was yelling at our men, who were all sullen and silent. "I know Rowe is fast, but you have to play man-on-man."

"I'm trying, but I can't keep on him, Coach," Henry shouted to be heard over the boos of the Raptors fans. Totally deserved boos.

"Let me play," Aarni barked up at Terri, who glanced at me with a frown. I'd let Aarni play only when Tennant Rowe's line wasn't on because I simply did not trust my player enough to let him hit the ice with his nemesis out there. There was no way in hell I would be party to an incident like the last one with Aarni and Tennant. He could bitch all he wanted. He could report me to the players' union. He could call me names. He could even keep dropping nasty comments about cheap hotels and pretty rich bottoms. I shook my head, and she continued shouting at the lines who were catching their breath.

I stood there, insults and jeers raining down on my head, and followed the next moment of play with a keen eye. Our young defensemen were just clearly outmatched by Rowe and his line. But perhaps we needed to juggle things a bit and see if instead of trying to defend a phenom, we could shove our hotshot rookie up the Railers hotshot vet's ass.

"… dominate board play and—" I stepped into Terri's play discussion, which was something I normally did not do. "Coach?" she asked, staring at me in confusion.

"I want our second line out there against their first line," I said and then smiled at the look that Ryker Madsen gave me. It was part terror and part joy.

"Yes, Coach," Ryker barked, swinging his leg over the boards. Alejandro and Sam Bennett rounded out the second line and were ready to go. I gave Terri and Art a smug wink. We were down by four. Either we pulled the goalie, which still might happen if Colorado didn't find his mojo, or we put new faces into that monster of a line the Railers had.

Rowe smiled at Ryker when they approached the faceoff circle. I leaned up and glanced down over the heads of my men to find Jared Madsen. Or was it Madsen-Rowe now? Whatever. The man was always cool as a cucumber behind the bench, but I did see a bit of a glowing admiration on his handsome face. Watching his son—who was the highest-scoring rookie in the league and destined to be going to the All-Star game come voting time

—lining up against his husband must be a rush of about ten million emotions.

Leaning back, I folded my arms over my chest, gave Terri a nod, and then let the hockey gods work their magic. The next two minutes was perhaps some of the greatest offensive hockey I had seen in many a year. Right from the faceoff, which Madsen won by shouldering his stepfather out of the way, to the shot on goal that Colorado kicked out of the way with the end of his skate, then back to the other end where Ryker took a flaming cross-ice pass from Garcia that got him a sneaky little shot that made the massive Russian goalie, Stan Lyamin, flash some serious leather to rob the kid of a goal, it was all poetry in motion. Like ballet on skates.

Then something went awry, and the small jolt of momentum we had been getting with the rush of young blood fizzled out. Actually, it was more of a wet raspberry than a fizzle. And it all happened because of a hothead goalie who thought he was still standing in the spotlight of center stage. I would have liked to have pinned it on Aarni, who was out on the ice with his defensive partner now that the Railers' fourth line was out, but nope. This one all came down on Colorado and his famed temper. Aarni and Adler Lockhart were scrapping it out in the corner for the puck. Adler got it free, skated around the back of the net, and tried to tuck the puck in. The wraparound attempt failed. Colorado had his skate firmly to the post, and the puck was held to the ice by Penn to get the whistle and stop play.

Lockhart, who was known for talking all the damn time when he was on the ice, said something to Penn. It seemed to be a chirp of some sort, for Lockhart's quirky smile was evident. Whatever he said incensed Penn, and our goalie took a chunk out of Lockhart's chin with his stick. Whistles blew. Penn shoved Lockhart, who was bleeding like a stuck pig. The Railers gathered around our goalie and began pushing. Aarni and the rest of the Raptors, raced to Penn's defense. When it was all sorted out, we had a double minor to serve. The Railers' power play unit took the ice, and within fourteen seconds, the captain fed the puck to the superstar, and he took a shot on one knee that put the puck high and over Penn's shoulder. The puck hit the crossbar and bounced into the net. Rowe leaped to his feet and pumped the air. Penn beat the crossbar with his stick until it shattered, and the fans threw the evening's giveaway—little stuffed raptors now minus their heads—onto the ice.

"Jesus H. Hairy Christ," I snarled, wondering if we would ever reach thirty-five points by my cutoff date. If not, Mark could send me packing, which I didn't think he would do now that we were fucking like rabbits, but his motherfucking brother Cam would in a heartbeat. I tossed Art a glower. "Tell Andre he's going in for the rest of the game and will get the start for the next one against Los Angeles."

Art nodded and went to our backup goalie, the young Andre Lemans, who nodded briskly. We managed to limp through the second half of that four-minute fiasco without being scored on again. When we filed off at the end of the period, I rode up hard and fast on Penn, taking him to the side and explaining to him that this was not the fucking Roxbury or Studio 54, which got me a look of confusion.

"Doesn't matter. The point is that this is a team game. You're not the fucking star here on this stage. You're sitting out this game and the next."

Penn's outrage was only matched by his shock. "*What?* That's bullshit! What he said to me needed a reaction!"

My eyes narrowed. Had Adler Lockhart said something homophobic or racist? I had a hard time thinking that anyone on the Railers would get nasty. Not with all the rainbow tape, flags, stickers, and *Love is Love* radiating from them.

"What did he say?" I'd fight for my men if someone slung a slur at them. The Railers' dressing room was just down the hall. I'd go find Lockhart and take him to the rug if he—

"He called me a Barry Manilow wanna-be!" Penn seethed, his pine green eyes snapping. "Fucking soft pop shit music. I'm a metal singer!" He pounded his chest with his blocker.

For fuck's sake. "No, you're a hockey player who won a spot on this team. *My* team." I leaned in close. I could smell the sweat and anger and stench of hockey pads rolling off him. "I don't care if someone calls you Liberace, you do not act out and draw a penalty. You see Lyamin losing his cool?"

"He's a crazy damn Russian who talks to his fucking pipes!"

"Well, maybe *you* need to take up talking to your pipes or the ice or your damn skates. Whatever it takes to keep you in control and in the game. I fought hard to get you on this team, Colorado. Don't make me regret that."

He bit back whatever it was he was going to say. "Yes, Coach," he mumbled instead, spinning around and stamping back to the Raptors' dressing room. I drew in a long, calming breath. One of the Raptors' equipment managers hustled past, pulling a cart of clean towels behind him, whistling a Christmas tune. The one about rocking around a Christmas tree. Rocking and rockers were on the bottom of my twinkle lights and candy cane list right now.

"Ho-fucking-ho," I whispered to myself as I stalked to my office to grab a Dr Pepper and calm my own ass down.

The next two days off were calling loudly. Perhaps Santa would bring me a trip to the Gila Monster Motor Court, a way to rid my bench of a festering sore of a player, and a fitting comeback to someone calling you a Barry Manilow wannabe to pass along to my metal-worshipping goalie. Things couldn't possibly get much worse, of that I was sure.

FIFTEEN

Mark

I WAS COUNTING down the hours until I finally got to meet up with Rowen, only first of all I had Christmas with the family in the big old Westman-Reid mansion, with Mom presiding over what so far had been a good day. Apart from missing time with Rowen, that was. The motel room was block-booked for the entire two days we had off, and even though my skin crawled at the thought of what bugs might be sharing our room, the lure of sex and time with Rowen outweighed the cons.

"This is for you, Uncle Mark."

I took the brightly wrapped gift from Lewis, who stood expectantly in front of me. He was a lovely kid, very much like I remembered Jason in a lot of ways. Quiet, thoughtful, but passionate about his interests. He loved Lego to the point that every one of his presents was Lego. I recalled Jason had once owned the biggest collection of *Star Wars* figures in the entire world. Or at least it had seemed that way. On one Saturday afternoon, stuck indoors with strep with the rain pouring down outside, Jason had even let me play with him. I could remember

Jason demanding that I played all the Wookie parts. Funny I thought about that day because Cam and Leigh had joined us, and the four of us had all kinds of amazing made-up adventures in Jason's room.

"It's a book," Lewis said and waited for me to open it.

"Don't tell him!" his sister, Deborah, shouted at him.

He rolled his eyes, in that patented big brother way, and yep, that was a mini-Jason standing in front of me.

I made a show of shaking the gift, then carefully untied an entire roll of curling ribbon before pulling out a photo book. The minute I saw it, I could feel my chest tightening. I don't know who'd made the book, who'd chosen the photos, but I wasn't ready to take a trip down memory lane.

"It's pictures of all of us," Lewis said with excitement. "Look." He took the book from me and turned a few pages, then sat next to me on the sofa. There wasn't much room, so it was a tight fit, but I couldn't help but love the way he leaned in on me, trusting that his uncle Mark wouldn't care. Steeling myself for what I was going to see, I looked down at the open book.

There was a photo of two children. A toddler holding a baby who was propped up by cushions.

"That's me an' Deborah," he announced, then reached over to turn the page. "And this is Annie and Monica, when they were born."

Annie and Monica were Cam's kids. Both of them favoring Cam's wife, Ailsa, who was stunning and always smiling. How could someone as angry and closed off as Cam have produced such gorgeous kids? The book carried on, images of the children from the day they were born right up to a few weeks ago. The last photo was of my three nieces and one nephew, holding up a sign "Welcome Home Uncle Mark." Something stuck in my throat, a ball of emotion that I couldn't shift, and I smiled down at the photo.

"I love it," I said and proceeded to receive hugs from Lewis, Deborah, and Annie, with a wet sticky kiss from Monica, who'd only just turned three. Monica stayed on my lap, cuddling in with the stuffed animal I'd bought her for Christmas. Of course, I'd also given my brothers cash gifts for all four of them, to invest for their future, but then I'd gone out and bought something for each of them myself. A stuffed dog for Monica, dolls for the other girls, and a Lego set for Lewis. Sue me if I'd stuck to gender stereotyping, but I didn't *know* the newest parts of my family so well.

I caught Ailsa's gaze and gave her a smile and mouthed a thank you.

She, in turn, thumbed at Cam, who was resolutely not looking at me at all. "Cam did it," she murmured, and at his name, he turned, and for a moment our gazes locked. He nodded. I copied him, and in that brief moment, there was a connection between us. It was up to me to build a bridge, I knew that, but I hadn't wanted to do it in this mausoleum of a house, with the ghost of our father looming over us. Then again, a person couldn't choose when and where to make things right with their brother.

Mom was the last to open a present. It was a book similar to mine, but it was filled with photos not just of her grandchildren but of her children, and there wasn't one photo of Dad in there.

I knew that. I checked as it was passed around. And Mom cried, but then when we all thought we were done, it seemed Mom had one last present for all of us.

"I'm in remission," she said, through tears, and although that word didn't mean much to the little ones, they picked up on her joy and everyone's excitement. Even

I was happy because I was coming to realize that I loved my mom. Right down in the darkest parts I'd hidden away when Dad threw me out, there was love for her and my siblings.

Presents done, we dispersed into smaller groups, the kids hyper, Mom and her daughters-in-law sitting and chatting, Leigh leaving the room to take a call, which left me, Jason, and Cam standing in the kitchen, each armed with a beer.

"He's called Leigh again," Cam said grumpily.

"I like him," Jason said.

"Who?"

Cam huffed. "Leigh is seeing this football player. Yeah, you heard, a freaking football player. A player with more money than sense."

"Who?" I queried, although from Cam's narrow-eyed expression I could tell that it was seeing and maybe more.

"Dean Hendersley, plays for the Cardinals, and yeah, I think it's serious. He's taking her away for a post-Christmas break."

"That's great," I said with a lot of enthusiasm.

Cam stared at me and then sighed. "Yeah, I guess he's a nice kid," he finally admitted.

"He's older than you," Jason pointed out.

"I need details." I decided. After all, I was home for a year. I should be able to play protective brother, right? Jason laughed then, which made me laugh, which meant Cam joined in. We all stopped abruptly, and Cam looked right at me.

"Shit, Mark," he muttered.

"I'm sorry," I blurted.

Then, in the cold kitchen of the big heartless house, we hugged.

And everything was beginning to right itself in the

world of the Westman-Reid brothers.

ROWEN PICKED me up a little after nine in the evening. He'd spent the day with Terri and a couple of the players, and the plan was we would go find a spot in the motel, fuck each other's brains out, and celebrate Christmas sated and sleeping.

Only I didn't want that.

For one, in my great brotherly love hugfest, I'd come to a decision without even realizing it. I was staying the full year. I was making the conscious choice to stay here, and it wasn't just to be close to the family or to work with the team. There was Rowen as well, in all his snappy, confident, toppy glory. I more than liked the prickly man. I certainly *loved* sex with him. I wanted more of the liking and the loving, and that was the weirdest feeling of all.

Worse than that, I couldn't imagine not seeing him each day—making it clear when I visited him in his office that I wanted his company. He never sought me out, but he never turned me away. And it wasn't always kissing or sex. Sometimes it was me bringing him a can of that evil-tasting Dr Pepper shit, or it was him making me eat something when he said I looked tired.

Of course I was tired a lot. I was juggling responsibilities for the agency in New York, along with the worries about money and the Raptors. I was also having regular mind-altering breathtaking sex. Any guy would be tired with all that going on.

"Where to?"

I realized he hadn't restarted the car, parking it at an angle next to the front gate to the Westman-Reid mansion and waiting.

"Are we not…" *going to have sex in a sleazy motel?*

"I have my own place. I mean, it's a rental, but it's mine. I even have a bed that has clean sheets on it."

He said that so seriously, but cleanliness was an important thing, and after some of the stuff we'd seen at the motel, fresh sheets sounded fabulous.

"Your place?" I wasn't questioning the statement, more the intent behind it.

Rowen crossed his hands on the steering wheel. "Damnedest thing happened today," he began. "I was at Terri's, and a couple of the team were there, and we were relaxed, chilled. Or at least they were as chilled as they could be with their coach sitting right opposite them." He laughed then. "Actually, Alex spent most of his time trying not to engage with me. Think he spent a lot of time in the kitchen making nonalcoholic mojitos that he never drank. I'm not *that* scary, right?"

"Says the man who made the entire team run up the steps to the top of the arena and then back down. Five times in a row."

"You have a point." He smiled then, and it was the most beautiful smile, and I wanted to tell him I wanted more than just a motel. Even if it was only for a year. I wanted to wake up next to him and make breakfast and sit naked in bed with him talking TV shows or music or feed each other toast and bacon.

"They respect you and fear you at the same time," I said.

"Yeah, so I'm sitting there, sipping this god-awful fake mojito, listening to Terri and her friend chatting about how they wished they were in the Bahamas, and I had a moment." He glanced out the front window, at the dark skies, and stared thoughtfully. "I don't want to go to the motel today."

Disappointment coursed through me. I knew it wasn't something that was going to last. I'd been fooling myself if I was—

"I'd like this to be something better than that, back at my place, with clean sheets, breakfast in the morning, talking, and not just sex."

Oh. Words escaped me, and I stared at him, probably looking like a complete fucking idiot, and I saw the moment that he was saddened I didn't say anything, then the moment when his expression changed and he smiled again.

"I'll take your silence as a yes, then?"

We leaned toward each other and kissed awkwardly until he pressed a button and his seat went back. I clambered onto him, getting caught on the console, yanking at my shoe, losing the shoe, nearly kneeing him in the balls, and then flailing as I lost my balance. He caught me and held me in a close hug.

"I'm too old for car sex," he said and took another kiss.

"Then let's get back to your place." I scrambled back to my seat, retrieved my shoe, and then clapped a hand on his thigh. "Drive!"

He took his sweet time pulling off from the gate, but as soon as we were out on the empty Christmas Day roads, he followed the speed limit, and we made good time back to the apartment complex that I knew a lot of the players rented in.

We stopped and kissed each other every few feet or so.

"I got you a present," he said between kisses.

"I got you one as well," I admitted.

"Mine is stupidly sentimental," he said.

"Mine too."

We stopped walking and stared at each other, and I wondered if I looked as blown away as he did.

He cradled my face with his hands. "Are we…?"

"I think we are." I rubbed my cheek against his hand.

We almost made it inside, got right to the lobby entrance when the door slammed open, and Alex was there, wide-eyed and pale. He shouted out a stream of Spanish, and Rowen waved a hand in front of him.

"Say again in English."

"It's Henry. I couldn't stop him. He agreed to go, and he wouldn't listen to me." He vibrated with tension.

Rowen snapped into coach-mode, gripped his upper arms. "What happened?"

"Henry went with Aarni. He'd been drinking." Alex shook himself free. "I should have tried harder to stop him. I had hold of him, but Aarni… oh God, he was drunk, and he got in the car, and Henry said it would be okay."

"Calm down—"

"Alejandro, listen to me." Rowen shook him a little.

"The car, there's been an accident. I don't know anything else."

Rowen took full control then. "What hospital?"

"I don't… I…" He scrambled to get his phone out of his pocket and held it up to us. "Twitter," he said helplessly. There was a picture of what was left of Aarni's orange-and-black Bugatti.

I took the phone and scrolled through the posts. "Fuck," I said as I read the tweets that speculated this was a car belonging to "that guy from the Raptors," and one of the photos caught an ambulance leaving and another one of the same ambulance arriving at the hospital. "He's at Memorial."

We were back in Rowen's car in seconds, Alex in the back, and reached Memorial within twenty minutes of leaving the apartment complex. We headed straight for the emergency room, not knowing what else to do.

"They won't tell us anything," I said as we stood in the middle of the waiting room. People stared at us, the three wide-eyed men wondering what the hell to do next.

"Coach."

We spun to see Aarni gesturing from a side room and went straight over. He closed the door behind us in what was clearly some kind of relatives' room.

"What happened?"

He didn't have a scratch on him, although there was blood on his left sleeve, and he looked as if he was in shock. He also stank of alcohol, like he'd opened a bottle of whiskey and poured it all over him.

"It's Henry. I shouldn't have let him drive." Aarni hid his face from us. "Fucking kid didn't know how to drive. Crashed it."

"*You* were the one driving!" Alex said, shocked and rigid.

"You don't know what you're talking about," Aarni snapped.

"I saw you," Alex shouted. "I saw you get in the car."

Aarni shoved Alex back against the wall, an arm to his throat, and for a moment Alex was still. Then with a twist, he was away from Aarni's hold, and it was Aarni pressed to the wall.

"Have you killed him? Have you hurt Henry?"

"He drove my fucking car into a brick fucking wall!" Aarni shouted back at him.

Rowen yanked Alex off of him and held a hand to Aarni's chest to stop him from moving. "Talk to me, Aarni," he demanded.

Aarni wouldn't meet his gaze, and I exchanged looks with Alex, who was bright-eyed with temper, his hands in fists. Would Aarni really let Henry drive his car? Had Henry crashed it? That didn't sound right at all.

"He could have killed me," Aarni said, but something was off. "What if I'd died?"

"I saw you drive away," Alex snapped, "and that's what I'm telling the cops."

Aarni ripped free of Rowen. "You punk-ass kid, you need to fucking go home where you come from—"

"Enough," Rowen said and got in between them. "Alex, sit down. Aarni, tell me everything."

Finally, Aarni glanced up, and in his eyes, I could see the same calculating look that my dad had been so quick to use. Aarni was working an angle, gauging the situation, deciding what to say.

"Kid's in surgery, and he might not make it," Aarni said with no horror in his voice at all.

Alex let out a keening cry and scrubbed at his hands, sliding down the wall into a crouch.

I sank into the nearest chair. I'd seen the photos, the way the car was mangled. Henry had been in that? We'd only talked the day before yesterday, after he'd scored a goal against Toronto, one of our best wins to date. I liked Henry, and now he was dying?

"The kid demanded to drive the car and I knew the car was too much for a kid like that. It's a man's car, for fuck's sake."

He was overdramatic, sneering, and none of this was ringing true. Henry was cowed by Aarni, under his spell, I'd seen it for myself, and wouldn't demand anything.

"He never wanted to drive your car!" Alex shouted and stood.

Rowen put himself between the two men again. "Alex, do you have a number for Henry's parents?"

Rowen had one hand on Alex's chest and the other on Aarni.

Alex's expression was full of pain, and he fumbled with

his phone. "What do I tell them?"

It wasn't as if any of us knew if Henry was even alive, and Rowen shook his head. Alex closed his eyes briefly and then left the room, shutting the door behind him.

"We should ask for news," I said, even though I knew that no one here would release details to a hockey team, even with one of the owners and the coach asking for news. The three of us sat together in one corner, Rowen quiet, introspective, me not being able to make sense of what had happened, and Aarni with his arms over his chest, looking as if he had nothing to worry about.

"Were you driving the fucking car?" Rowen asked him and leaned forward, his elbows on his knees.

"No," Aarni said, but his expression betrayed him. I knew what a liar looked like, and Aarni was lying. His eyes darted around the room, his fingers fisted, then loosened, and his brow was peppered with sweat. The door opened, and I expected Alex to walk in, but it was a cop, flanked by two security guys.

I stood immediately, as did Rowen, but Aarni was slower to stand, and I thought I saw fear in his eyes.

"Mr. Aarni Lankinen?" the cop said. "We have a few more questions following on from your statement."

Aarni cleared his throat. "I don't know what I can add. My good *friend*, Henry, took the car without asking. I managed to get in the passenger seat at the last moment, but he was driving like a lunatic and drove straight into a wall. I'm lucky to be alive, and now he could be dying."

"You're lying," Alex said from behind the security guards. "I watched you climb into the driver's seat. You barely made it. You were so freaking drunk."

Aarni tilted his head and sighed. "I don't know how much you could have seen from an apartment on the opposite side of the building to the cars—"

"I followed you down, you fucking asshole." Alex dashed forward, one of the guards catching him.

The cop was assessing the situation, his lips tight, his eyes narrowed, and then he nodded sharply.

"We have a report from the firefighters who responded to the call. It would appear that there is some confusion as to who was driving—"

"They're wrong," Aarni blustered, but I could see the small fear in him had become something else. He looked as if he wanted to run.

"Then I'm sure we can clear this up," the cop said.

Aarni spun to face me, gripped my shirt, uncoordinated and swaying, the scent of alcohol too much this close.

"Don't let them question me. I'm not going," he pleaded.

Rowen reached over and unpeeled his fingers before standing between me and Aarni. "What did you do?" he asked the hockey player.

"Nothing. It wasn't me. It was Henry. He made me do it."

Alex yelled something, the guards scrambled to stop him coming into the room, Aarni shoved at Rowen, attempted to push past the cop, yelling something, hitting out, but it was Rowen and the cop who finally subdued him, and he was cuffed. I caught Alex and held him tightly, even though he had weight and height on me. He appeared to be broken.

"Everything will be okay, Alex," I lied.

Alex's voice broke. "Henry could be dead. My friend could be dead."

Rowen sat back on his heels. "What did you do, Aarni? What the fuck did you do?"

SIXTEEN

Rowen

THERE WERE a few moments left until sunrise, and here I was, alone, at my patio door, staring at Spikes McGhee. I opened the slider gently and stepped outside. The air was cool, not Ontario-in-January cool, but cool enough to feel good on my bare feet and chest. My skin pimpled in goose bumps. Okay, so perhaps it *was* close to Ontario-in-January cool. I stood in the morning air, arms folded, looking up at the white hat atop my cactus buddy as the sky blossomed into a glorious palette of sangria, heather, plum, and flamingo-pink. The sunrises here were breathtaking on a nearly daily basis. My gaze moved from the oil painting Mother Nature was creating and settled on that white hat.

"You okay?" Mark asked groggily, appearing behind me on silent feet. He slid his arms around my middle and rested his scruffy cheek to my back.

"You know what a white hat symbolizes?"

"Something to do with computer hackers?" He yawned and snuggled close. His warmth crept into my chilly flesh. If only it could seep into my cold bones.

"Perhaps, but I was thinking more along the lines of

morality. In the old days of black-and-white cinema, the bad guys always wore black cowboy hats and the good guys white. It's probably some sort of cultural hang-up about white symbolizing purity."

"So we're standing out here half-naked when it's forty-two degrees, discussing the cultural conceptions of sexuality and gender?"

I exhaled deeply. "I veered off course. My point was that in the old westerns, the good guys wore white. When I moved out here, I thought I would be the good guy. I'd be a cowboy riding in on my trusty steed, white hat on my head, and I'd clean up this here town."

"May I say that you trying to sound like some cowboy right off the Texas plains with that Canadian accent is kind of funny?"

"No, you may not." He snorted softly and hugged me a little tighter. "I failed my team, Mark. I failed them by not getting rid of Aarni sooner. Now we have a promising young player in the hospital facing who knows how much rehabilitation and heartache, a media nightmare, and a team shaken to its already wobbly core. I failed them all. I'm no gallant sheriff with a shiny silver star."

"Whoa, okay, just whoa." His hold loosened, and he circled around to look at me. God, he was pretty with his hair on end and the purple pink of a new day on his face. Even with the shaggy whiskers and bags under his dark eyes, he was stunning. And my guts twisted like a politician's promise. "You're not responsible for any of this." I grunted and scowled. "Make that face all you want —it never did scare me. This whole damn nightmare rests solely on the shoulders of Aarni Lankinen and the owners of the team." I began to protest, but he steamrolled me. "Don't bicker. You're not responsible. My father is, for signing that motherfucker in the first place. Dad was the one who let Aarni stay on the team after that grisly attack on Tennant Rowe. My brothers and I are responsible because we dicked around and never made the hard call to look into getting rid of that poisonous scum as you asked. This whole thing rests on Westman-Reid shoulders, not yours. You did all you could do in the capacity that you had to work within. So don't be trying take the blame. I carry it, and I will fix things."

A whirlwind of emotions swirled around me, buffeting my heart and mind and soul, the gust of realization nearly blowing me off my feet.

"You're not nearly as intimidating as you like to think you are," I eventually said.

"Neither are you."

"You're also not nearly as vapid or self-centered as I originally thought." I cupped his face, his whiskers rough and erotic on my palms. "My experience with men like you…" He quirked an eyebrow. "Men who look like you. Who are too handsome to be real—models, actors, singers, the fashionable elite, you know, men like you. Every single one that I've ever met has been snobs. Every single one that I've dated has been insipid, greedy, uncaring dicks who cared more about Instagram followers and social events than the poor, hungry, or marginalized."

"I resent being clumped into that category," he stated, and I kissed him into silence. When he opened his mouth to protest again, I merely kissed him harder. "You can't kiss me forever," he snapped, his hackles clearly up. This was not going how I had planned. "Just because I modeled does not mean that I'm—"

"I know. I know. Please, just… can you let me finish?" I still held his face in my hands. His nose wrinkled in consternation, a look that was at once adorable and utterly prince-like. "He not only broke my heart. He shredded it."

"He who?"

"Not important. Please stop interrupting, or I'll have to kiss you again."

"Will you tell me about this jerk sometime?"

The man was ridiculously persistent.

"Yes, sometime, but not now, so please just let me get this out, or I will kiss you into submission."

"You need to work on your threats."

"Noted. So, this night… this horrible night has made me realize two important things. One is that I cannot save this team by myself. The other is that I love you."

The tension around his eyes and mouth disappeared as my confession sank in. Those dark brown eyes I enjoyed staring into softened and warmed.

"I'm not sure I like having a tragedy being what jolts you into seeing how marvelous we are as a couple." He rose to his toes to steal a soft kiss. I held his face, tasted of his mouth time and again, and then let him drop back to his feet.

"Sometimes it takes a tragedy to make a man wake up and see just how short life is and how little control he has over fate. Can we do this? This thing we have?"

"There really is only one way to find out," he replied, curling into my chest, my hands sliding from his cheeks into his hair. I carded my fingers through the thick mass, my heart beating strongly. His fingers rested on my lower back, warming the cold flesh. "I'm willing to give it a go."

"I'm not an easy man. I tend to be a little headstrong."

"Do tell."

"Also, I don't take directions well."

"No? *Really?* I hadn't noticed."

I wanted to say more, perhaps get into a little verbal back and forth, but I was just too miserably tired and upset. Eyes closed, I breathed him and the morning in, exhausted beyond belief, terrified of a future that I didn't control nearly as well as I'd thought I could. I lowered my lips to his hair, kissed the knots that his fitful sleep had made, and watched the sky brighten incrementally for several peaceful minutes.

"I'd like to give it a go as well. A slow go?" I pulled back so that I could look at him.

"Slow is fine. I know you're a bit wobbly when it comes to those pesky feelings."

I should have probably argued with Mark, but he felt too good in my arms, so I cinched him closer, craving the flesh to flesh and enjoying the first skinny ray of sun touching on Spike's white hat.

"You think maybe this town needs more than a lonely sheriff? I have a big gun if that helps you decide."

Mark slid free of my arms, grabbed my hand, and lifted it to his lips. "I think this town is going to need a whole posse of white hats. I'd be honored to ride at your side, Sheriff."

I captured his mouth and danced him back inside through the doors, his sleep pants coming off as soon as we were inside. Mine followed in short order.

"Deputy Princeling, that has a fine ring to it," I whispered beside his ear as I tugged him down to the couch, the love that had burst free for this man beating against my ribcage like a newly fledged bird.

"I want a damn badge," he countered, tumbling to the sofa. I fell over him, nudging his legs apart, lowering my mouth to his. "And a horse named Winston Hundertwasser the Fourth."

He bumped and pulled at me until we shuffled around with me, dropping my back to the sofa. My skull bounced off the arm.

"Ouch," I mumbled, although the pain was negligible.

"Your head is hard. You'll be fine," he replied, his lips brushing my throat.

"Stay."

Hold me. Love me.

"Pushiest sheriff in the West," he replied.

More like neediest sheriff in the West.

"Okay, you get to wear the deputy badge," I said when he nestled into my arms and spread his lean, hard body over mine. Nightclothes were never worn when we were in bed or on the sofa as the case may be. I liked… no, I *longed* for his flesh pressed to mine.

He snickered softly, kissed my throat, and reached over to find a blue-and-brown western throw that lay draped over the back of the couch. Once we were wrapped up in it, he drifted off, his head under my chin, and I lay there, wide awake, my hand on his back, my sight on that white hat sitting jauntily atop a cactus. Maybe something good could come from this horrible mess that the Raptors were now facing. Hoping for some kind of miracle, I let sleep ride down on me like Pat Garrett on the trail of Billy the Kid.

———

SLEEP LASTED for two and three-quarter hours. Not nearly enough. Two cell phones chirruping at the same time a foot from our heads roused both of us. My neck was stiff from the odd angle of my head on the arm of the sofa. Mark pawed around on the coffee table, answered the wrong phone first, then chucked my cell at me as I worked my head in slow circles after kicking off the cover to sit up, my spine cracking ominously. Who his call was from, I could only guess. Jason. Mine was from Terri, and she sounded as cracked and broken as the rest of us.

"Hey," she said, the exhaustion weighing down her usually peppy disposition. "So, they just brought Henry back from surgery. He's going to be fine. They think. Eventually."

"Thank God." I ran a hand over my face. I needed to shave, shower, and eat, then get back to the hospital to see Henry, if I could. Probably his parents had flown in from the Midwest by now. Where was he from? Illinois? Iowa? Fuck, my brain was slurry. I wondered how Ryker was holding up. He and Henry had grown pretty close, sharing a house and all. Christ, this was such a miserable fucking mess.

"… whole list?"

I found my way back to the conversation. Mark had risen and was now pacing, chattering with animation and anger to our general manager. "Sorry, I was drifting. List of what?"

"Henry's injuries."

"God. There's a list?"

"As long as the injury list after the Cup finals are over."

Sweet baby Jesus. "Sure, tell me."

And so she began rattling off poor Henry's injuries—broken sternum, shattered kneecap, broken femur, bruised lung, concussion, cracked ribs, possible whiplash, and an eye injury that she'd not been able to ferret out the severity of. The broken bones would heal, given time. Henry was young. The concussion would also fade. Eye injuries, well, those could make or break a hockey player's career. It's damn hard to control a puck if you can't see out of one eye.

"… family is here now. Rowen?"

"Yes, yes, sorry. I'm beyond tired."

"I feel you. Look, I'm going to round up the rest of the rookies here and shuttle them all home, but Ryker and

Alex are refusing to leave. I'm about to pull out the big guns, so you need to back me up. We do have a game tonight."

Yes, we did. Against Dallas and Tate Collins. Heaven help us. "Good girl." She coughed discreetly. "Oh no, woman. No, coach. Not girl. Apologies. Get them home and into bed. Tell Ryker and Alex that is a direct order from me. I'll be there in an hour or so."

"Rowen, the police have Aarni."

I glanced up at Mark circling my living room like a shark. "Well, of course they do. That's management's worry. Ours is the team. Send out a text on the team chat. Morning skate is canceled, but I want them at the barn thirty minutes earlier than normal. We might have updated information on Henry to pass along to them. Don't tell them that, though. Just tell them—"

"I'm on it. Why don't you go back to sleep? Henry's family is here. You'll probably not get in to see him anyway, at least until they move him from critical care."

"I want to speak with his family. Just get the kids home and don't worry about me. I got my deputy. Things will be fine."

"Your deputy? Rowen, have you been drinking and talking with that stupid cactus of yours?"

"No." You had a friend/associate coach over, got wasted on the tequila she'd poured down your throat and had an in-depth conversation with a saguaro cactus in a hat one time... "Just get home. Thank you for manning the fort for a few hours."

"Did you get any rest?"

"Enough. See you later. Drive carefully."

"You too, Coach."

I ended my call, stood, and padded into the bathroom to

piss and shave. Mark arrived as I was smearing shaving cream on my cheeks. His mouth was set, his eyes red-rimmed, and his hair flat to the side of his head, which had lain on my shoulder.

I lowered my foamy hands from my face and caught his eye in the mirror. "How bad is it?"

"They're going to charge him with a felony."

"Christ."

"Yeah, I don't think even having the legal team looking out for him will help." He placed his phone onto the counter, uncaring that I'd splashed water all over the place. "His blood was full of narcotics and alcohol. He's broken about twenty Arizona traffic laws, caused severe bodily injury to the passenger and to public and personal property, and tried to harm one of the arresting officers as they walked him into the police station. Handcuffed and all, the stupid dick tried to head-butt a cop. I just…" He tossed his hands in the air. "What do you do with a man as stupid as he is?"

"Sell him to some Russian league?" I picked up my razor, gave my face a hard swipe, and hissed at the sting of blade removing skin along with whiskers. "Motherfucking bitch."

Mark's eyes went round as the hub caps on a '53 Packard. "Oh, shit! Don't panic. Let me get some clothes on, and I'll get you to the emergency room!"

"Mark, stop, it's okay." I grabbed the hand towel and held it to the cut along my jaw. "I won't bleed to death. Honestly, it's okay. It's not a large cut or deep. It's just superficial. Give it ten minutes or so, and it'll stop."

He stepped closer to rub a hand up and down my back. "Are you sure you don't need anything? That nose spray that you use for your disorder?"

I removed the towel, frowned at the blood welling up—

cuts on the face and head always seemed to bleed longer than anywhere else—and reapplied pressure.

"Nope, I'll just wait, and it will clot. It will."

He seemed disinclined to believe me, but fifteen minutes later, when the nick was mostly done oozing and a Band-Aid had been applied, the worry lines around his brown eyes lessened.

"I am seriously going to need a drink before this day is over," he said, stepping into the shower with me to wash my back because he seemed to think a shaving nick meant I was unable to scrub my own ass. Whatever. I was happy to have his hands on me in any capacity. And his concern? That was nice too.

"What's management doing about Aarni?" I asked as hot water pounded down my back. Mark was in my arms, his back against the tiles, his hands resting on my hips, his lips gently pressed to the tiny bandage on my jaw.

"Providing a lawyer, paying his bail, and meeting in an hour at the arena to discuss his future with this organization. Then the owners will join you at the hospital and speak with Henry's family to offer them any kind of support, mental or monetary, they may need to help them and their son through what will be a lengthy and difficult recovery."

I dropped a kiss to his sodden hair. Guess old man Westman-Reid had been right during that sales speech he'd given me. Most things in Tucson *were* a joy to hold. Well, he'd said *be*hold, but holding felt better. Add in prickly yet beautiful, and I had the man who had stormed his stubborn way into my heart.

SEVENTEEN

Mark

WE HAD OUR PRIORITIES. Rowen wanted to check in on Henry and understood that I would have to leave and deal with Aarni, but when it came down to it, I went with Rowen to the hospital. Jason and Cameron were in with the lawyers, but somehow I felt closer to the team and to Rowen, and I needed to be there.

We paused just before Henry's room in silent agreement and took a breath, not knowing what we'd see or find behind the closed door.

"Are you here for Henry?"

We turned to face the man behind us, who looked so much like Henry that he had to be related.

"William. I'm Henry's dad."

Rowen held out a hand immediately. "Coach Carmichael."

William nodded. "I know who you are," he spoke quietly and held a hand out to me.

"Mark Westman-Reid. I'm—"

"Right," William said and dropped my hand as if it was burning him. He tilted his chin and looked right at me.

"You want to explain why you didn't drop Lankinen the moment you arrived?"

What was appropriate for me to say here? Should I explain that we wanted him to go, that it wasn't us that had kept him, but that we didn't have options.

"I'm sorry." *How lame is that?*

He shook his head. "You have no idea, do you? Henry has been skating since he was old enough to strap on skates. He's wanted *nothing* in his life but hockey, and when he was offered a contract with the Raptors..." A nurse hurried by us, and he dropped his voice. "I was so proud."

"As you should be," Rowen murmured. "He's a good player. He'll go far."

William's expression was bleak, his eyes glassy with emotion. "He might not walk again. How do you expect him to play?"

The words were brutal, and I wished to hell I could say something that would make this better. "The Raptors will pay for the best care, the best rehab—"

William rounded on me. "He doesn't need your money. We're fine."

A woman joined William, her eyes red with tears, her face puffy. "William, we need to talk to the doctor." She didn't even bother with introductions. She was lost in that place of grief where nothing and no one could intrude.

We watched them walk away, and it was only when Rowen pushed Henry's door open that I followed him in and shut the door behind us. I didn't want to see. I didn't want anyone else to see. Not watching the machines or following the tubes running to Henry's body or hearing the steady beep of the monitor. I wanted to protect Henry, keep him safe. Rowen went to the bedside immediately, and I hovered a little way back. Henry lay in a slightly elevated bed, his eyes open, his skin white, and bandages on his head, his neck, down onto his chest, his leg in a cast, and in his hands the control of a morphine drip.

"Coach," he whispered, his lips dry and his voice raspy.

Rowen held some ice chips to Henry's mouth, and Henry blinked up at him as he took a chip with his tongue. "Henry, hey," he murmured.

"Sorry, Coach," Henry rasped, and his voice cracked.

"Nothing to be sorry for. No more talking now. I want you to know that the place on the team is open for when you're fit to come back."

Henry cried silently, a track of tears that slid down his cheeks and to one side. Rowen wiped them away with a tissue and cradled the part of Henry's face that wasn't marked or covered in white. "Everything will be okay," he murmured and smoothed a thumb over Henry's cheekbone.

I backed out of the room. I shouldn't have been there. I should've been organizing healthcare or finance or talking to the cops or organizing that buyout shit so we could dump Aarni. Anything but stand there watching the bond between coach and player.

The sitting area outside the private room was heaving with flowers, and I went to the first of the bouquets, reading the words that people sent. Some were from fans, a couple from teams, and others that looked like they were from family. The biggest, most extravagant bouquet was from someone called Adler Lockhart. Whoever this Adler was, it was clear Henry meant something to him.

"What are you doing here?" I turned to see a young guy who could have been Henry's twin.

Holding out my hand, I stepped forward "Mark—"

"We know who you are. What are you doing about Aarni?"

"He's in police custody right now—"

"You make him pay. Don't you take him back, not after what he…" The man collapsed into a chair as if his strings had been cut, the huge bouquet tumbling into him. I stopped it from falling, but the card slipped out, and the Henry-lookalike picked it up.

He snorted a soft laugh and turned it over to read the message, then bowed his head. "Adler says he's here for us. For all of us."

"Good," I said because the quiet needed to be filled.

Henry's door opened, and Rowen stepped out.

The newcomer stood immediately. "Coach Carmichael," he said, and they shook hands, then did a complicated bro-hug, which made me think they must have known each other really well.

"Dan, God, I'm sorry we're meeting again under these circumstances." He pulled back. "Mark, this is Dan, Henry's brother. I coached him at the University of Western Ontario."

Oh, so that explained that.

"Talking of Western Ontario, that idiot Adler sent this," Dan waved at the huge flower arrangement.

Rowen shook his head ruefully. "He never knew when to stop at college, and he still doesn't now, even with an NHL contract under his belt."

"The Railers are lucky to have him."

For a second the two men seemed lighter, but it didn't last long.

"You know we're keeping his place on the team, for however long it takes," Rowen said much more seriously.

"Yeah, right. What does team management say to carrying Henry like that?" There was so much pain in his voice, and he stared right at me.

"*Management* will support Henry and his family until the moment he is capable of making a decision about his future, based on discussions with Coach Carmichael and medical experts. We will honor his contract to the letter."

Dan narrowed his eyes a little, not looking as if he believed me.

"Mark is one of the good ones," Rowen said, and I felt pathetically grateful for the distraction.

WE MADE it to the arena with two hours to spare before the game, not stopping to talk to journalists at the gate and splitting up when we got in. Now we had separate things to do, and I had to pull up my big boy pants and start dealing with the Aarni mess.

Cam and Jason both glanced up when I went in. Our lawyers were there, huddled over paperwork, and even Leigh and Mom were sitting at the window, staring out at the view, talking quietly to each other.

"And?" Jason asked, which got Mom and Leigh's attention and unfortunately the lawyers as well. I had a freaking audience, which was hard to handle at the best of times. I was used to people staring at me from back in my modeling days, but right now, I didn't want anyone looking at me.

Because let's face it, I felt I was about to lose my shit.

"Henry came through the operation . Time will tell what he can and can't do. Meanwhile, I haven't had any news about Aarni, so I can't help you there."

Cam and Jason exchanged glances. "He's been arrested," Cam said. "Bail is one million. He's posting it himself, and he's already given an interview talking about judgment calls."

"He said he was led astray," Leigh muttered and stopped next to us. I sat down to be more on her level, and thankfully everyone else did, which I was glad for because my legs felt like jelly.

"Tell me he didn't say he'd been led astray by Henry? What the hell?"

"We're selling the house," Mom said, and I moved my head so fast I swear I gave myself whiplash.

"We're doing what?" And when I said we, what I meant is *you* because the house wasn't ours. It was Mom's to do with what she wanted. Not that I cared. I hated that damn house.

Cam cleared his throat. "The money will be invested in the Raptors and will assist in carrying the debt for Aarni's buyout."

I inhaled sharply and let out a noisy breath. "We're doing this, then?"

Jason held my gaze and gave me a half smile. "We're all in if you are, little brother. We can use all the help we can get. The fans hate us, the sportswriters despise us, and the league is one step away from tar and feathering us. You've proven you're a hell of a businessman and can handle our headstrong coach. I might have a friend who can give us a hand with social media and our packaging and marketing. So, what do you say?"

All in? Past the year? Staying here in Tucson?... I looked over at the assembled legal team and then at each member of my family. Mom looked strong, had color in her cheeks, and I needed to connect with her again. I loved Leigh and wanted to get to know her enough to have a brotherly say in who she dated so I could be annoying. Jason was the sensible one, and I respected him, and as for Cam? He'd really been my best friend as well as my brother, and I could do with some of that in my life right now.

And Rowen. I had Rowen. I wanted Rowen. I wanted my family to love Rowen.

Abruptly I had the insane thought of placing my hand out so we could do a family huddle but managed to restrain myself.

"I'm in," I said. "All in."

THE NEWS HIT social media about ten minutes before the Raptors were due on the ice against LA. This was a local derby for all intents and purposes, one of our nearest teams. Well, certainly nearer than New York or Toronto. None of the team would have phones. I knew for sure that the staff wouldn't, so it was me on my own in the damn box who saw it first. Or at least along with those in the rest of the arena who were checking scores and posting selfies.

Millionaire Hockey Star Pleads Guilty

The picture was the Raptors head shot of Aarni, the news brutal and to the point. There was a short postscript about Henry, who after two weeks was still in the hospital and likely to be there for a couple of more weeks to come. He was healing physically, but I had no idea where his head was at. Rowen visited him, said he'd be moving back home to Illinois with his parents, who were still threatening to sue the Raptors for duty of care, although they hadn't done so yet. I guessed that would come from Henry when he was capable of making decisions. I didn't think we'd even defend it; just let the insurance companies duke it out. If it had been up to me, I'd have given Henry everything, but the guilt I felt was nothing compared to what Alex felt. He still blamed himself for not stopping Aarni driving off with Henry, and Rowen told me his game was suffering. He was benched tonight, for stomach flu or some such nonsense, according to Rowen, which of course left us a good man down, and Ryker without his two wingmen in Alex and Henry.

"At least he's stopped protesting his innocence," Alex said, startling me out of my thoughts as he sat next to me. "I can't believe he's gone this long pretending the evidence is all lies."

"I guess your stomach's better?" I deadpanned.

His lips quirked in a wry smile. "Yeah, I fucked up," was all he said.

The noise in the arena rose—I guessed a lot of fans were reading the same news. There was some booing, shouts, and Alex gave a full-body sigh, then shrugged and slumped in his seat. "Should be on the ice right now."

I could nod or make a noise of encouragement, but I didn't think that was what Alex needed right now.

"Yeah, you should." He looked surprised. "You need to stop messing up and be there for Ryker and the team. They've lost three straight games, and you've been a waste of resources down there."

Temper sparked in his eyes, and then vanished in an instant, and he scrubbed at them hard before leaning his elbows on the glass.

"I can't stop thinking about it," he said after a short pause. "I should've been able to stop him."

"Shoulda, woulda, coulda. We, we all do things we regret, but Henry wouldn't want you messing up the lines because you can't keep your temper in check. I swear with you *and* Colorado—this team is angst city."

He huffed. "I'm nothing like Colorado. He's just a rocker head case."

I leaned on the glass next to him. "Yeah, but he's down on the ice at least."

"Touché," Alex murmured, and then there was no

more talking as management and extras came into the box, including Robert and Clark from the car dealership. They headed right for me, shook my hand.

"Contracts are in place to be signed," Robert said.

"Told you as soon as Aarni was gone, we'd sign." Clark shook his phone. "and I guess you now have no choice but to get rid of him, right. Right?"

They were looking at me and wanting a reply. "There is no place for Aarni with the Raptors. Yes, he's gone."

We won the game four to nothing, including a hat trick from Ryker and Colorado with a shutout. I shouldn't have worried that the news about Aarni was going to shake the team. It seemed they were energized by the news that must have reached them through the grapevine. We'd all been waiting for him to stop this mess from going through the courts, hoping to hell that he wouldn't defend his position that he wasn't in the wrong. God knew what kind of deal he'd made to get to this point, but we could finally breathe a sigh of relief.

"I'll be on the ice next game," Alex promised me, or himself. It wasn't obvious which it was.

As soon as I was able, I went down to the press room and waited for Rowen to take his seat for Coach's Corner, hoping that seeing a friendly face might make any awkward questions easier to take. Jason spoke first before Rowen even got there.

"The Raptors organization is aware of this evening's news. Coach Carmichael will not be discussing the matter further."

There was a small ripple of disappointment, but no one said anything out loud. When Rowen took his seat, the questions were innocuous, talking about Alex being a healthy scratch, about Ryker and his strong slapshot, about Colorado being a brick wall.

"Coach, the team is at twenty-five points, and we're only three weeks from the All-Star break. Is that the count what you wanted for your first season in charge?"

Rowen sought me out then, and our gazes locked. So much passed between us that I wanted to run up to hug him and reassure him that everything was going to be okay.

"I was hoping for a minimum of thirty-five points by midseason, but circumstances being what they are, I see a stronger second half of the season for us. This team is strong. We have some key players and good chances."

I'd forgotten about that damn point clause. If the Raptors didn't hit it, then we could invoke the clause to get rid of Rowen and hire another coach.

Emotionally, that thought killed me. From a business standpoint, management and the owners would've been stupid to take him away from a team that showed flashes of brilliance like tonight. The Raptors needed a chance, and with Aarni gone, maybe, just maybe, with positivity and hard work this rebuild could become a miracle.

I waited for him in his office, and as soon as he shut the door behind us, he walked straight into my arms, and we hugged.

"Congratulations on the win, Coach."

"Did you see Ryker? And Colorado? So much potential."

"I spoke to Alex. He knows he's fucked up."

"I hoped you might talk to him. That's why I sent him up to the rich boy box."

He kissed me then and cradled my face.

"I love you," he whispered against my lips, and I smiled.

"I love you back."

Epilogue

FOURTEEN SECONDS LEFT, and we were down by two. As the clock ran out, I gave myself the rare opportunity to take a moment and just be pissed off right there at the bench.

"We'll get them next time," Terri said as the team shuffled off the ice, heads down, wallowing in another loss. "The All-Star break will do us all good. You going anywhere?"

I looked down at my eternally perky associate coach as we trundled down the corridor behind the team. How did I answer that exactly? We had failed to reach that thirty-five point caveat I'd slapped into the contract, when I'd been so damn cocksure of my abilities.

"We'll see," I replied, moving past equipment managers and press, eager to get to home.

A text came in from Mark as I was slamming around inside my office. I ignored it, unable and unwilling to drag him into my foul mood. Without a glance back, I was out the door, stalking to my car and driving home with a thundercloud over my head. As soon as I got to my place, I stripped down to my underwear, grabbed a six-pack of Dr Pepper from the fridge, and threw my sorry ass onto the couch to watch movies, sulk, and try to come up with a plan B now that plan A had spiraled out of the sky in flames and crash-landed with a massive explosion, eradicating my future plans and my ego. BOOM.

I'd not been home fifteen minutes when the front door swung open and in strolled Mark, dressed in cool desert colors, with a damn shopping bag dangling off his arm.

"Why did I give you a key?" I asked, before cranking up the volume on the movie. He strolled over, sat down, and wrenched the remote from my hand.

"Because you love me," he countered, turning the volume down so he could be heard. "Is that a talking Gila monster?"

I blinked at him. "It's Smaug. Last great dragon to exist in Middle Earth? Invaded the dwarf kingdom of Erebor?" He shrugged. I shook my head. "How are we even a couple?"

"Oh, it's a dragon. I don't do dragon movies. Too unrealistic." He hefted his bright red shopping bag up to his lap and leveled inquisitive brown eyes at me. "I texted you. Did you not get it or did you have your phone off?"

"I got it. I just didn't read it."

"Mm, okay, I see. So we're pouting." He tried to turn the movie off, but a small skirmish over the remote broke out, which I won.

"No, I'm not pouting. Children pout. I'm ruminating." I crossed my arms over my chest, hiding the remote neatly up by my armpit.

"Ruminating. Of course, so you're now a goat. What exactly is it you're ruminating? And why does that short man have such big, hairy feet? Oh, I know him from

Sherlock. I could spend hours staring at Benedict Cumberbatch."

"Are we here to talk about your thing for British men, or are we here to talk about me?"

"You're extremely petulant tonight. It was only a loss, Rowen. We're all prepared to see lots of losses for the next few years before the rebuild work is done and we're a contender."

"I didn't make my self-imposed point goal," I reminded him as if he didn't know all of this. He nodded in silence. "I'm disappointed in myself. I feel as if I—"

"I know what you're going to say. You let the team down, you let the fans down, you let the press down, you let Henry down, you let the people who cook the hot dogs and sell the beer at the games down, you let the stray cats who roam the trash cans outside the arena down, you let the—"

"Okay, I think you've about covered everything." I so wanted to huff and sulk, but as I'd pointed out to my boyfriend, grown men didn't sulk or pout. We just acted like assholes. My sigh was deep and heartfelt. He gave me that damn "just-so-you-know-I'm-right" smirk that I loved/hated in equal measure. "I should have answered your text. I thought if I had a night alone to contemplate and work out my discontent, I'd be in a better place tomorrow when I met with you and the other heirs to end my tenure here."

"Oh, that. Yeah, I took care of all that during the game." He rummaged around in his shopping bag as I stared at him in confusion. "You know it gets kind of boring up there in the rich-boy box as you like to call it."

"Am I off the mark?" I mean, it *was* a rich-boy box, and he *was* a princeling.

"No, not really. Anyway, we were losing, and I was

bored, so I broached the subject with the family, and we decided that we'd need more time to see if you could reach your full potential. So we scribbled out this silly little waiver and signed it, which we will present to the stockholders and our legal team." He handed me a napkin that had a small smear of mustard on the corner. I held it under my nose, then drew back when the words were blurry. "You really should get your eyes examined. I think you'd be sexy as fuck in reading glasses."

"Hush now. I'm reading." I held the napkin out at arm's length and skimmed over the gibberish and scrawls. Then I looked at Mark. He was quite smug. "This is indecipherable."

"Well, we'll get it typed up and neat, all legal-like before we send it to your agent, but basically it says that we feel more time is required to implement your new program and that letting you go now would only set us back."

"And how long do you think you'll need to see if I can bring this bunch of junkyard dogs to heel?"

"At *least* four years," he replied primly, his lips twitching and his eyes alight with mirth. "Unless you're set on leaving now, which would sadden us all greatly."

I placed the napkin beside me on the sofa and craned around to look right at him. He was the prettiest man I had ever met. Saltiest too. Tastiest as well.

"Did you push for this extension because we're lovers? If so, I'm not going to accept it."

His eyes rolled so hard I feared they might tumble out of his head. "Rowen, honestly, do you think I don't know you well enough by now to know better than to try something like that?"

"I had to ask." I did have my pride. I'd not be kept around simply because one of the owners loved to suck my dick.

"Of course you did. And the answer is no, we are not making this offer of an extension because you and I are in love. We're making this offer because we have faith in you, your vision for this team, and the new system that you're implementing. Change takes time. We know that, and we wish to give you all the time you need to get this team turned around. So you can ruminate on that as well tonight and let us know in the morning. Now, onto the other goodies."

He stood, smiled, and began taking off his clothes, item by item, until he was gloriously naked. My gaze roamed over all that sweet, bare skin. He bent over and tugged two white ten-gallon hats from his big red shopping bag. One he plunked on my head, the other he placed artfully on his. He took a moment to get the hat at just the right jaunty angle.

"As you can see, we're now the law in this here town." He dropped to one knee, then swung a leg over my lap, his pert ass resting on my thighs, his mouth a mere inch from mine. "You're the sheriff, obviously, because you have a spiffy star on your hatband. I'm the new deputy, and I have no idea how to deputy a hockey team, but you're madly in love with me and will do your best to show me the ins and outs of deputy work." My hands roamed along his ribs, then settled on his lower back, a smile toying on my lips. He rocked up and back, tempting and teasing, his breath fanning my face. "I think the first thing you need to show me, Sheriff Carmichael, is how to handle that big, fat gun of yours."

"The first thing I need to show you is how much I love you." I leaned up just a bit to capture his mouth. He settled against me, chest to chest, and kissed me back. "Good thing I've got four more years. I think it might take me that long to show you properly."

His lips moved over my face, soft little kisses raining down on my mouth and chin and nose, making me wriggle and twitch.

"Then we'd better get started. Show me how much you love me, Sheriff."

"Yippee-Ki-Yay."

THE END

Next for the Raptors

Across the Pond (Raptors 2)

The greatest journey isn't from England to the States, it's the one that two men take on the way to find each other.

Sebastian Brown is on a mission to rescue the Arizona Raptors and a vow he made to a friend in college. Either that or he's on vacation. He's not entirely sure that he's made up his mind yet. Either way, traveling from England, to the arid desert of Arizona isn't exactly a picnic, particularly with the doubts and worries he takes with him. He's turned even the worst of companies around, but faced with the challenge of improving the reputation of a hockey team that everyone seems to hate, he knows his work is cut out for him.

Focus is key, but that is easier said than done when Seb is sent into a tailspin by the intriguing Alejandro. Seb's entire marketing plan hinges on making Alex a poster boy for equality and fair play. But with Alex's utter dedication to the game, and his dark secretive eyes, the gorgeous Alex is stubborn, opinionated, doesn't want any part of being the team focus, and worst of all, doesn't appear to like Seb at all. It takes everything that Seb has to keep his hands off of Alex, but things get out of hand and Seb's life might never be the same again.

Alejandro Garcia has had to work hard to get where he's at. Born to Mexican immigrants, his siblings and himself have never had it easy in this new country their parents dreamed of calling home. A native son of Arizona, Alex has always been the odd man out on the ice but he's not going to let a stupid thing like his heritage get in the way of his dreams. He's now a Raptor and he plans to put all that training and collegiate hockey experience to good use. Working hard comes naturally to him. It's something his parents have instilled in him from the time he was a toddler. Being one of a handful of Latino hockey players makes him strive for success with even more determination. His first pro season has had some ups but a lot more downs, but Alex is one stubborn young man and failure is not an option.

As the Raptors struggle to rebuild not only their team but their core values, Alex finds himself drawn to one of the owner's friends, a tall, lanky Brit with the face of an angel and an accent and attitude that bewitches and befuddles him. Sebastian is everything he thought he would never be attracted to but he can't push the sexy, older, fun-loving man out of his thoughts. If ever there were a man he would not be able to take home to his parents - not that he can bring a man home since he is deeply closeted - it's Sebastian, but desire knows no socioeconomic, age, or international borders. The heart wants what the heart wants and Alejandro's wants Sebastian.

Hockey Series' from RJ Scott & V.L. Locey

Harrisburg Railers

Owatonna U Hockey

Arizona Raptors

Boston Rebels

LA Storm

Chesterford Coyotes - Young Adult

Harrisburg Railers

When hockey wunderkind Tennant Rowe meets his new coach, he knows he's in trouble. Jared Madsen is nine years older than Tennant, impossibly attractive, and — worst of all — his brother's off-limits best friend. Is their chemistry worth the risk?

Changing Lines (Railers 1)

Can Tennant show Jared that age is just a number, and that love is all that matters?

The Rowe Brothers are famous hockey hotshots, but as the youngest of the trio, Tennant has always had to play against his brothers' reputations. To get out of their shadows, and against their advice, he accepts a trade to the Harrisburg Railers, where he runs into Jared Madsen. Mads is an old family friend and his brother's one-time teammate. Mads is Tennant's new coach. And Mads is the sexiest thing he's ever laid eyes on.

Jared Madsen's hockey career was cut short by a fault in his heart, but coaching keeps him close to the game. When Ten is traded to the team, his carefully organized world is thrown into chaos. Nine years his junior and his best friend's brother, he knows Ten is strictly off-limits, but as soon as he sees Ten's moves, on and off the ice, he knows that his heart could get him into trouble again.

Changing Lines

Harrisburg Railers (Hockey Romance)

1. Changing Lines
2. First Season
3. Deep Edge
4. Poke Check
5. Last Defense
6. Goal Line
7. Neutral Zone
8. Hat Trick
9. Save The Date
10. Baby Makes Three
11. Rivals
12. Perfect Gifts
13. Family First

Railers Volume 1 | *Railers Volume 2* | *Railers Volume 3* | *Railers Volume 4*

Owatonna U, College Hockey

Meet the men of Owatonna University's hockey team

Ryker (Owatonna U, 1)

Ryker

Ryker is hockey royalty, Jacob is a poor country boy. Can two vastly different people find common ground and become the men they want to be?

Ryker comes from a long line of championship-winning hockey players. Playing college hockey to develop his game is his only focus, and nothing will stand in the way of him working to become the best player. He has no room for relationships, people who point out his flaws, or anyone who calls him on his dreams.

He certainly has no place for love, and meeting Jacob is nothing but a useful distraction on the side. After all trying to get his Owatonna Eagles teammate into bed is less work and more play. When tragedy rocks his family, his charmed life crumbles, and the only person he can turn to is the same one who claims to hate him.

Jacob Benson has only known hard work and stifling conservative values his whole life. Born and raised in the small rural community of Eden Crossing, Minnesota, he's the only son of a hard-working but struggling dairy farming family. Jacob is using his skills in hockey to finance his way to an agricultural science degree. These four years at Owatonna U. will probably be the only time he has to enjoy life, gain acceptance about his sexuality, and live openly before his inevitable return to the farm. Running into a pretty rich boy like Ryker Madsen is putting a damper on his enjoyment of life away from home. Ryker's flip, conceited, carefree attitude grates on Jacob's every nerve. So why, if Ryker is everything he dislikes, does he want nothing more than to explore the sinful dreams that his annoying teammate stars in every night?

Ryker

Owatonna U Hockey (Hockey Romance)

Coast to Coast (Arizona Raptors 1)

Coast To Coast

When opposites attract, this bottom-of-the-league team will never be the same again.

A stipulation in his father's will forces Mark back into the arms of a family that disowned him and leaves him one-third owner of a hockey team facing financial ruin. He doesn't even watch hockey, let alone like it, and wants nothing more than to head back to New York. Then there's the new coach, a stubborn, opinionated, irritating man with superiority issues and questionable music taste. Butting heads with Rowen becomes the new normal, but it comes with passionate debate and an all-consuming lust.

Challenged to rebuild one of the worst teams in the league into a future cup contender, Rowen can't pass up the opportunity. Never in his twenty years of hockey has he ever seen a team managed so badly or coached players overflowing with resentment and bigotry. Yet there's something about this team and this city that compels him to roll up his sleeves and start dismantling. If only Mark, one of three siblings who now own the Raptors, wasn't so damned rock-headed yet so damned appealing his job might be easier. It doesn't look like either is willing to give in, but one night in a dark, desert hotel changes everything.

Coast To Coast

Arizona Raptors (Hockey Romance)

1. Coast To Coast
2. Across the Pond
3. Shadow and Light
4. Sugar and Ice
5. School and Rock

Top Shelf (Boston Rebels 1)

Top Shelf

Acting on the attraction to his best friend's brother has always been off the table for Xander until a passionate hookup with Mason at a beach resort begins a love affair that burns long after summer ends.

Mason specializes in assisting same-sex couples on their journey to becoming parents and fighting every rule that blocks his way in the stuck-in-the-past agency that hired him. Living in his brother's pool house is rent-free, and every cent he earns he saves for his dream—that one day he'd have his own company helping others. The downside is that he has to see his annoying brother every day, the upside is that his brother's teammates from the Boston Rebels make regular visits. The eye candy that passes Mason's window is almost enough to make him consider dating a hockey player, but not just any player though. Ever since Xander —his brother's childhood friend—came out as gay at a press conference, Mason's puppy love has turned into a burning attraction he can no longer ignore.

Hockey has been one of Xander's main focuses since he was old enough to balance on skates. Well, hockey and Mason Kingsley, but Mason was always unattainable. Now that he's about to see thirty candles on his birthday cake and is no longer hiding the fact he's gay, he's ready to find a soul mate to make his life complete. A summer vacation is just what he needs to have time to think, but when the Boston Rebels arriving in paradise with Mason in tow, thinking is the last thing he needs. One torrid night under a balmy moon and rules about not messing with his best friend's brother vanish on a warm, tropical breeze.

Summer romances don't generally last past Labor Day, but with the new season about to begin Xander and Mason are going to have to face the world and decide if their love is real enough to withstand everything.

Top Shelf

Boston Rebels

Lost In Boston (Free Prequel Novella)

1. Top Shelf
2. Back Check
3. Snowed
4. Royal Lines
5. Blade

6. Rental

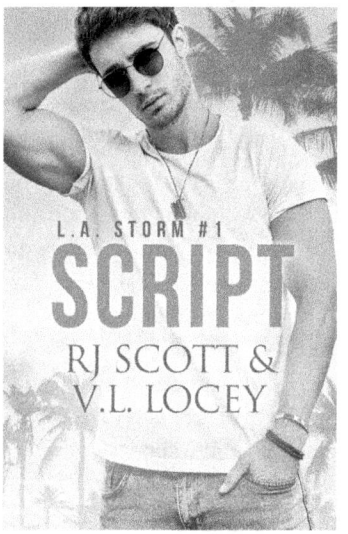

Script (LA Storm, 1)

Script

Hollywood A-lister Finn might be Canadian, but he needs Cameron to show him how to hockey.

Actor Finn Kerrigan is at a crossroads. After growing up a soap star, then starring in a hugely successful trilogy of action movies, he's finally given the chance to read a heartfelt and passionate script that could change his life forever. The role would be enough for people to see him as a serious actor, and maybe even win him an award or two (and no, a golden raspberry award for his action movies doesn't count). Once established as a serious actor he's sure he can come out of the closet and finally live his truth. When he lies to get the part of a hockey player on a struggling team, he suddenly has nowhere to hide. He might be Canadian, but the last time he skated he was ten, and no, he doesn't have hockey in his blood. With only a month until filming starts, he about to be exposed, but partnered with a player who's supposed to be giving him tips, he doesn't realize how many of his secrets will come to light. Falling in lust, one heated kiss at a time, is inevitable, but giving Cameron up at the end of the shoot could break his heart.

Cameron Chavkin is the face of the LA Storm. And the body, and the hair, and the smile. He's at the prime of his career, men and women want to be with him, and he's skating better than he ever has before. His house sits next to a famous rock star's mansion, his garage is filled with expensive cars, and he's even been asked to mentor a once-famous actor in a new hockey movie. Life is pretty sweet. Until the bad boy of hockey meets Finn, a man on the edge with more secrets than Cameron has endorsements. Knowing better than to get involved, Cameron is swept up despite himself, and when it's time to say goodbye to the Storm's most eligible bachelor is finding it hard to follow the script.

Script

LA Storm

Off The Ice (Chesterford Coyotes, 1)

Off The Ice

**A coming-of-age love story with high school, hockey
rivalry, friendship, family, and coming out.**

Soren's life changes in an instant when he and his younger
brother are adopted by hockey royalty. Making sense of his new
life is hard enough, but when he's enrolled in a private school it
means facing a whole new set of problems. Navigating friendship,
family, and hockey is one thing, but being attracted to the boy
who vexes him is a whole new thing.

Felix has a reputation to protect. He's the kid who seems to have
everything but looks can be deceiving. Spinning lies about his

perfect life, he's created a fantasy world that even he has started to believe. Only, it's not long before everything crumbles, all of his pretty lies are revealed, and only his closest rival sees through his pain and stands by him.

Fighting is easy, friendship is hard, but love is everything.

Off The Ice

Chesterford Coyotes

1. Off The Ice
2. On Thin Ice
3. *Dance on Ice*

Also By RJ Scott

For a full list of ebooks and links please scan the code above or
visit rjscott.co.uk/rjbooks

Meet RJ Scott

RJ discovered romance in books at a very young age and realized that if there wasn't romance on the page, she could create it in her head. With over one hundred and fifty books published, she is a full time author of gay romance.

She lives and works out of her home in the beautiful English countryside, spends her spare time reading, watching films, and enjoying time with her family.

The last time she had a week's break from writing she didn't like it one little bit and has yet to meet a box of chocolates she couldn't defeat.

www.rjscott.co.uk | rj@rjscott.co.uk

NEWSLETTER - rjscott.co.uk/rjnews

facebook.com/author.rjscott

x.com/Rjscott_author

instagram.com/rjscott_author

amazon.com/author/rj-scott

bookbub.com/authors/rj-scott

goodreads.com/rjscott

pinterest.com/rjscottauthor

Also By VL Locey

For a full list of ebooks and links please scan the code above or
visit vllocey.com/stories-from-vl-locey

Meet V.L. Locey

V.L. Locey loves worn jeans, yoga, belly laughs, walking, reading and writing lusty tales, Greek mythology, the New York Rangers, comic books, and coffee.

(Not necessarily in that order.)

She shares her life with her husband, her daughter, one dog, two cats, a flock of assorted domestic fowl, and two Jersey steers.

When not writing spicy romances, she enjoys spending her day with her menagerie in the rolling hills of Pennsylvania with a cup of fresh java in hand.

vllocey.com
vicki@vllocey.com

Newsletter - vllocey.com/newsletter

- facebook.com/V.L.Locey
- x.com/vllocey
- instagram.com/vl_locey
- bookbub.com/authors/v-l-locey
- goodreads.com/vllocey
- pinterest.com/vllocey